Christmas
To Jean:
Light your candle of hope!
Jeannine Dahlberg

Candle in the Window

Jeannine Dahlberg

1663 Liberty Drive, Suite 200
Bloomington, Indiana 47403
(800) 839-8640
www.AuthorHouse.com

This book is a work of fiction. People, places, events, and situations are the product of the author's imagination. Any resemblance to actual persons, living or dead, or historical events, is purely coincidental.

© 2005 Jeannine Dahlberg. All Rights Reserved.

No part of this book may be reproduced, stored in a retrieval system, or transmitted by any means without the written permission of the author.

First published by AuthorHouse 06/27/05

ISBN: 1-4208-5837-8 (sc)

Library of Congress Control Number: 2005904485

Printed in the United States of America
Bloomington, Indiana

This book is printed on acid-free paper.

To my daughters Heidi and Erika,
whose enthusiastic support was greatly appreciated.

And

To my brother Fred, a Korean War veteran,
whose military experiences are reflected in this story.

Also by Jeannine Dahlberg

Riding the Tail of the Dragon

CHAPTER ONE

Fingers, which were nimble, now tighten in a frozen grip on his M-1 rifle. Large, fluffy snowflakes gracefully flutter among bursting shells. The night sky is brilliant with flashes of light illuminating patterns of destruction from both incoming and outgoing mortar shells as they explode. Tracer bullets pelt the ground, ricochet at a forty-five degree angle upwards into the darkness streaming tails of light, then fade and disappear. His rifle squad of nine soldiers was deployed as skirmishers in the area hours earlier and they are scattered in a long line awaiting further orders to advance when reinforcements arrive. The enemy is hunkered down a few hundred yards to the north in the valley and he is dreading the inevitable skirmish.

Seth is so cold. He tries to forget the imminent danger and projects his random thoughts, which rumble around in his head, to a happier time when he and Rachel sat side-by-side on the Ramsey plantation in Virginia staring into the flames of a campfire planning their future together. As if in a daze of disbelief, he shakes his head discouragingly with the thought, *eight difficult months – no, a lifetime later and I am holed up, crouching low and waiting for I don't know what.* He shivers and thinks… *Korea is so cold.*

Has it been only eight months since he and Rachel embraced, pressing their warm bodies ever so closely together saying their last good-bye with passionate desire… wanting more, but hesitant.

Everything drastically changed when he was drafted into the army. He reminisced to the past summer when, after graduating college, he traveled around the world in search of a missing heiress, Rachel Ramsey, and found the girl of his dreams. Loving thoughts of Rachel trigger his memory and he quickly looks at his watch. It's midnight. He audibly mumbles words of apology to Rachel for missing the appointed hour of ten o'clock when each one will confess love for the other feeling that their souls will communicate. It was a warm thought and for a few moments Seth forgets where he is. He allows the luxury of a daydream to invade his conscious awareness for safety and drifts into a melancholy stupor. He closes his eyes, reliving the first time he saw Rachel Ramsey.

*****

The Ramsey Plantation was well known along the east coast as one of the finest tobacco plantations in Virginia. Over the years, its growth had expanded to include the commodities market and the banking industry… and much of its success could be attributed to the Colemans, who had been the caretakers and business managers for several generations. The Colemans took great pride in playing an active role in the plantation's development. Seth Coleman was born on the plantation as was his father BillyJoe and his father before him.

When the matriarch of the Ramsey family died, BillyJoe hired a detective agency to try to locate a possible sole survivor to inherit the Ramsey fortune. A baby girl, Rachel, was reported to have been born to the Ramsey son and his wife in Paris before World War II. The mother died at child birth and the son was killed, leaving the baby to be placed in an orphanage in Paris. It was presumed by BillyJoe that Rachel had survived the ravages of the War in Paris. After the detective agency failed to uncover any leads to locate Rachel, BillyJoe asked his son, Seth, if he would try to find her after he graduated college, and Seth jumped at the chance to bum around Europe over the summer before starting his career as an architect.

As if to relive the excitement of finding Rachel, his thoughts spill over with enthusiasm into each episode encountered, which brought him closer to her discovery. He mentally retraces his journey. After leaving his home on the plantation in Virginia, Seth's search for the missing heiress took him to Paris where he uncovered records of Rachel's birth at the hospital; found her mother's interment records at the cemetery; found the orphanage from where she had been adopted shortly before the outbreak of World War II by General Erik von Horstmann, of Hitler's Third Reich, and the family's frantic escape to Macau; and his meeting with Inspector LeCleur at Interpol, which necessitated his traveling to the Orient aboard a tramp steamer where he gained maturity in worldly matters of espionage. While the ship was at anchor in Victoria Harbor in Hong Kong, a small craft maneuvered along side to await a passenger to be transported to the island of Lantau. A young woman stood at the control of a sampan. She was strikingly beautiful in the morning sunlight as her lithe body gracefully moved with the motion of the sampan as it rode the waves in the harbor. She was dressed in the typical Chinese black trousers and loose-fitting jacket with her long blonde hair plaited in a queue, which fell down her back almost to her waist. It was a few days later when Seth discovered the beautiful young woman on the sampan was the missing heiress, Rachel Ramsey.

He believed it was destiny that played its part in bringing him to China where he found Rachel. After each series of harrowing events encountered, which brought him closer to her discovery, he believed the Oriental mystical powers and positive forces of feng shui were riding with him and protecting him on his journey. It was beyond his belief that he could be so lucky. He was thrilled when her father, General Erik von Horstmann, agreed that she should return to the States with him to verify the validity of her birth to the probate court so she could inherit the Ramsey plantation. They were together only a few short months, but those were precious days on the plantation where they fell in love. It was a time that seldom comes but once in a lifetime… a magical interlude, which will live in his memory forever. He felt it was paradise to be with her and to hold her close to him. With his eyes closed, he relives the exhilarating feeling of the warmth of her body close to his and the softness of her lips, which ignites lingering sensations arousing a sexual drive, and it is their last kiss that he now builds his dream with a heart that hungers for her touch. He quickly issues a prayer that he will continue to be protected while in Korea so he and Rachel can find happiness and build their lives on the strength of their love. He realizes they are from opposite ends of the world, though, and with a heavy heart and to his chagrin, she chose to return to China. There is a brief minute when there are no thoughts. He feels dejected, slumps on his rifle and whispers: *I miss you so much... it hurts.*

*****

A large burst from a mortar shell close by startles Seth to stark reality and he instinctively grabs his rifle to a firing position. His thoughts of Rachel quickly disappear as his rifle is now his best friend. The rapid staccato beat of his heart pulsates in a heavy chest making breathing difficult. He has been well trained in the technical skill of weaponry, but he has not yet faced the enemy in combat and his anxiety is overwhelming. A great feeling of loneliness overtakes him initiating fear. As if to console himself, his eyes and mind become sharp and alert to verify that the stretched line of nine soldiers in his squad is still in place. He knows he cannot let his rifle freeze from the cold; and with a possessive, protective grasp, he cradles the rifle in his arms and awaits orders.

Shaping in the shadows behind him, Seth discerns a large contingent of soldiers quickly taking positions along the hillside where the rifle squad is stationed. He gives a friendly nod to the approaching men and breathes a sigh of relief.

As if on cue, all Pandemonium breaks loose and in the din of confusion Seth realizes this is his first combat. He is stunned from the excitement and noise of battle and briefly becomes disoriented. He feels receptive to an out-of-body experience and draws upon his close infantry training in boot camp to sustain him while he fortifies his senses with quickness and precision to adjust to the possibility of hand-to-hand combat while he quickly affixes his bayonet. He is amazed and pleasantly surprised that his rifle appears to have a life of its own, which is well disciplined to combat and appears to be brilliantly reacting to his command. Together they are a well-trained fighting machine.

The shelling stops and flares begin to explode casting an eerie light. Soldiers from both sides rush toward one another into the open valley where mortal contact injects its sinister destruction upon fighting men. Seth is in the heat of the battle, dispatching death-dealing thrusts with his bayonet. The Chinese are far outnumbered in this skirmish and the bloody, vicious fighting ends quickly as many Chinese soldiers surrender.

The fighting at this time had become a type of trench warfare. American and allied troops were well above the 38th parallel and the North Koreans had relinquished their military role to the Chinese, who sent thousands upon thousands of men to fight. Peace talks were stymied and each side fought to control little pieces of real estate. In a state of denial, Seth looks around at the horrendous, bloody scene before him. He doesn't want to believe what men can do to each other. His hands tremble. The strength he miraculously had during the battle now ebbs, leaving him weak and drained of feeling. The fighting machine has shut down to a hollow shell of a man where rational thought humbles him to disgust for his part in creating this debauchery to humanity. His complexion pales and he becomes sick to his stomach. He looks upward toward the sky, knowing that the great vault of heaven has the answers to his perplexing questions. He knows that it is only through the grace of God that he has survived this close combat. Tears well in his eyes and he offers a prayer of thanks... and for forgiveness for the lives he has taken.

Seth briefly watches as prisoners are quickly hustled together. He controls his emotions, once again draws upon his strength and instincts for survival and proceeds to assist with the duty of guarding the prisoners. He is reminded of what he heard a month ago when he first arrived in Pusan, South Korea. The graphic story painted an indelible picture in his mind of our Marines becoming stranded at the Chosin Reservoir. The Chinese took no prisoners. A mismatched Army task force was deployed to support the Marine right flank, and many who survived the fighting withdrawal died from the bitter cold when temperatures dipped to twenty-four degrees below zero. Only a few men lived to tell the story and they are known as the Chosin Few. Seth has great respect for these courageous warriors.

He looks upon these Chinese prisoners with disdain and contempt for their atrocious actions at the Chosin Reservoir; but with ambivalent feelings, he is proud that his country shows civility in human propriety even to the enemy. In a philosophical mood and to strengthen his reasoning and purpose for fighting in Korea, he projects his thoughts to the necessity for war, where opposing forces struggle for a particular end for justification. He has been advised that the conflict in Korea is termed a "police action", but to the fighting men on the front line, Seth believes it looks and feels like war. In the face of his first mortal combat, he feels assured that he maintained his honor and dignity and did not feign from his duty as a soldier.

The long, arduous march back to the tent camp was uneventful. It was a welcomed sight to see the compound, which for now is Seth's home. The camp is completely surrounded by barbed wire fences with hundreds of cans dangling from the wire on short lengths of string, which when jostled will produce a cacophonous sound alerting the soldiers to any intruder who manages to infiltrate the grounds. Trip flares are strategically placed around the camp, which, when triggered, will light the night sky, along with booby traps and mines.

A few men were leaving the mess tent after breakfast amid the clanging noise of these dangling cans, as desperate, hungry people pushed one another into the wire, reaching for food the soldiers were throwing away from their mess kits. This was an everyday occurrence at mealtime when refugees from their bombed-out villages come in search of food. Newly arrived soldiers to the camp are quickly advised not to go near the barbed wire fences to give food to these hungry people as there could be guerilla fighters in the crowd ready to kill any soldier who ventures too close to the barbed wire. A quick thrust with a knife could take a soldier's life and the assassin could easily melt into the frenzied crowd. The military police guard the wire at all times. When Seth first arrived, it was his instinctive inclination to reach out to these people across the wire to offer food he was discarding, but he quickly learned there are times when caution must take precedence over passion if he is to survive in such a hostile environment.

CHAPTER TWO

Seth was happy to be back in his tent among his few meager belongings. It was home, and after last night, it never looked better. He was pleased to see his buddy, Ian, had made it back safely and was already asleep on his cot. He was anxious to talk to him about the skirmish, but he had second thoughts about awakening him as too many men were shot and killed by startling a sleeping soldier in his own tent.

With a deep sigh of relief and a guttural groan of exhaustion, Seth flopped headlong onto his cot. A nightmare of vignettes depicting the grisly battle the night before evoked a distressful rest; but finally after a couple of hours, his body and mind succumbed to a peaceful sleep when conscious awareness of precautionary senses is relaxed.

Seth was abruptly awakened by a commotion in camp. The loud yell of "mail call" always brought the men out of their tents in a festive, boisterous mood, and Seth was quick to join in the melee. This was the highlight of the day when every soldier hoped to get a letter or package from home… even advertisements or junk mail would be a bridge to home and could bring a smile to their face.

Ian quickly followed and called, "Hey, Seth, wait! Our bet is still on and I have a lucky feeling that I'm going to get a letter from Emily today, which means you will owe me one dollar."

Seth countered, "No, it's my lucky day and I'm going to get a letter from Rachel."

It had been over three weeks since Seth had received a letter from Rachel and he was beginning to feel concern for her safety in Hong Kong. He was not happy with her decision to return to the Orient, especially after the fighting in Korea had escalated to include the Chinese. He had hoped she would have wanted to remain in Virginia on her newly inherited tobacco plantation for the duration of his tour of duty. Then, after he was mustered out of the Army, they could marry and decide where they would want to live. It was her passionate pursuit to help and comfort the children in the orphanage on the island of Lantau that seduced her to return to China… an attraction so great that she relinquished complete ownership of her plantation, dividing half to its caretaker and manager BillyJoe Coleman, and she renamed the plantation Ramco. In her last letter, she had mentioned that many more children were starting to spill down the hills into the orphanage and she was happy with her decision to return to the compound on Lantau to assist with the children's needs, as the orphanage was poorly staffed.

Men jostled one another good-heartedly in an attempt to get closer to the postman as all were eager to get mail from home. Seth and Ian jokingly pushed forward into the crowd, exchanging nonsensical remarks with their buddies while awaiting their names to be called. Seth's worried expression on his face betrayed his true feelings and Ian asked, "Hey, man, you really are worried that you may not get a letter from Rachel. What's up? Did you two have an argument?"

"No, I'm worried she's back to leading a double life at the orphanage."

"What!" Ian exclaimed. "Just don't throw that at me without explaining it."

Seth continued, "After Rachel's father General Erik von Horstmann defected from the German Army to the Allies…"

"Wait a minute." Ian injected. "Stop right there. Explain how that happened."

"Years into the war, General Von, as he is called," Seth said in a low voice, which epitomized respect, "could no longer justify the inhumane atrocities of Hitler's Third Reich executing an exercise in genocide and wanting a complete annihilation of a race of people. The general was suspected of being one of the conspirators of high-ranking officers involved in an attempt to kill Hitler and it became imperative that he seek refuge." Seth and Ian continued to be shoved and jostled by the noisy soldiers who crowded closer to the inner circle around the postman. Seth spoke louder to continue, "With help from Interpol, he was able to contact the French Resistance. He advised he would supply information to thwart an attack on Churchill's life in exchange for safe passage for him and his family to Macau, which was recognized as a neutral country. His knowledge of the German army's tactical movements proved invaluable and his reputation as a brilliant military strategist was quickly recognized." The boisterous frolicking of the soldiers became too distracting for Seth to endure and with his right hand he pulled Ian by the arm to move a short distance from the inner circle. Seth was determined to finish the story. "Shortly after he and his family arrived in Macau, he was approached by both British Intelligence and the French Interpol offices to command the post in the Orient in the fight against gold smugglers and drug traffickers in the Hong Kong, Macau and Canton areas. He accepted the position and he and his family moved to the island of Lantau where the police compound was built after World War II. The idea of expanding the compound to accommodate an orphanage came quickly when Rachel's mother saw all the children coming out of the hills after the war to seek refuge.

"Rachel grew up in the orphanage, and at dinnertime would listen to the general and her mother discuss strategy procedures to combat the evil element in China. As Rachel would say, 'They became a tight threesome, where out of necessity to survive the hardships of World War II in France, they learned to depend on one another.' She repeated many times…'War is a brutal teacher for daily survival.' When she grew older, her father consented to let her participate in certain, safe confrontations with the Chinese Triad, mostly in a surveillance position.

"I pray she will keep her promise to me and will put that cloak-and-dagger work behind her. Already, she has put her life in jeopardy more than once. I'm even more worried now since Major Tamermia mentioned the other day that drug trafficking in the Orient has escalated to a greater and more serious level."

Ian was held spellbound and listened intently to Seth's story. The postman called his name twice… the second time more loudly… before Ian realized he should step forward to receive his mail.

Men lingered in the cold weather for a short while longer after mail was called, as some liked to see the joy expressed by those soldiers who received letters from home and could live their happiness vicariously.

Seth watched the men step forward to receive their mail, but his mind-set was on Rachel. For the past few weeks, too many plaintive daydreams were haunting his reverie and causing intuitive thoughts to be distressful. His anxiety was great as he stepped forward to receive his mail. He received a letter from the architectural firm of Joseph A. Gabriel and Son in Willmington confirming they would be happy to hold open his position with the firm pending his return from military service. He received a letter from his dad, BillyJoe, whose letters were always filled with an account of his struggles in managing the plantation. Seth could understand his frustration during World War II when gas and tires were rationed; and now with his dad's added responsibility of being a co-owner of the plantation, which included banking interests and the commodities market, BillyJoe worried if he could maintain and exceed the growth of the corporation to please Rachel Ramsey. Seth figured that with his dad's business acumen of increasing the wealth of the plantation over the past fifteen years, assuming a co-owner's position should cause no added anxiety and stress. He let it suffice his dad is just a worrier.

There were times when Seth felt sorry for his dad. The plantation was his life… his whole life. There had never been a respite from his responsibilities. BillyJoe was loyal to the memory of his father and grandfather before him who were the plantation's caretakers to remain steadfast in his service to the Ramseys… it was the Coleman's point of honor.

At the end of the letter, BillyJoe mentioned he was beginning to worry that he had not heard from Rachel in the past month and she was supposed to have returned the signed financial statements approving the fiscal report as quickly as possible to appease the auditors.

Seth reread the short paragraph over and over again, while his mind raced with possible reasons why he and his dad had not heard from Rachel... all reasons were spiced with premonitions of danger.

There was no letter from Rachel.

With drooped shoulders and in the depth of despair, Seth turned to Ian and slipped a one dollar bill into his hand. Ian was reading a letter from Emily.

CHAPTER THREE

Fear grips Rachel when she awakens to find she is alone and curled in a fetal position on a cold, damp stone floor. The small cell-like room smells of mold. Sunlight from a barred window casts shadows of the bars onto the adjacent wall and a huge steel door keeps the room secure. An iron cot with a dirty, thin mattress and a small water basin complete the grim surroundings. Her long, blonde hair falls across her face and she instinctively reaches for the black ribbon, which holds her hair back from her eyes in a braid. The ribbon is gone. She pulls at a knot of something in her tousled hair only to discover it is a large, ugly cockroach. Frantically, she flicks the cockroach to the floor and watches as it scampers to a crack in the wall where it disappears. Crying uncontrollably, her body quivers from shock of her predicament. After a few minutes, she reprimands herself for her actions and realizes she must stay calm and give rational thought to her situation. A physical inventory of her arms and legs reveals nothing is broken for which she is thankful; and other than a fiercely throbbing headache from a huge bloody lump on the back of her head, everything else feels okay.

She sits for awhile trying to recapture in her mind the circumstance that put her in this predicament. Her vague thoughts rumble around in her head with no decisive answers. Bewildered and with blurred vision, she rises to look out the window, hoping the view will look familiar, but the window is too high. The room swirls, her eyes roll, her legs crumble beneath her and she falls to the floor unconscious.

Many hours later, she awakens to the sound of men yelling outside her cell door.

"Don't blame it on me!" Chang yelled. "I wasn't the one who hit her on the head. When General Tso learns that you almost killed her, I wouldn't want to be in your shoes and…"

Wang interrupted, "Hold on, Chang, we did what we had to do to get her out of Hong Kong quietly and fast. She was screaming so loud I believe she could wake our dead ancestors. Let's see if she is awake now so we can turn her over to Sun Lo. I don't want to have to be in Tokyo any longer than necessary. I'm not happy when I am in Japan."

Again, Rachel is gripped with panic fear not knowing where she is or who has abducted her. Still dizzy, she crawls to brace her back against the wall while waiting for what or whoever will come through the door. Her eyes are wide focusing to see in the dark and not knowing what to expect when the door opens and two men enter… each holding a candle. Their voices are gruff as Wang pursues to question her in Mandarin Chinese.

With her hands outstretched and with a pleading look in her eyes, Rachel shakes her head from side-to-side indicating she does not understand. Her thoughts are rational enough to know that she should not answer his questions. She believes it will be for her safety if she does not indicate at this time that she understands Mandarin Chinese. When she speaks in English, Wang becomes agitated as he realizes they cannot communicate. He bends low over her… eyes glazed with wild, sexual lust and violently pulls her to him. With one hand he roughly yanks her hair back tilting her face upward to his and with his other hand he grabs the front of her blouse. Breathing heavily, he utters, "I know how to get what I want." Rachel fights pounding her fists, pummeling his muscular chest and screaming for help.

With the speed of a young cheetah, Chang pounces on Wang's back holding a knife to his throat and with clenched teeth growls, "General Tso does not want her harmed." The knife's blade cuts deeply into the skin as Wang quickly stands throwing Chang from his back. The two glare at one another for a few moments... each one sizing up the fighting ability of the other when they are interrupted by the sound of a Japanese guard approaching. Wang snarls, "I will not forget this!"

The flickering light from the candles play havoc with Rachel's ability to observe more closely her abductors as their features are immensely distorted by the candle glow. She focuses her attention on Chang, her protector, who has taken a position closer to the candlelight and for a brief moment her spirits are lifted as she feels she recognizes him. Her senses swirl in disbelief, but she can no longer concentrate as her thoughts, once again, become jumbled.

A Japanese guard enters the room and places a pan of food beside her on the floor and a candle on the windowsill. He gives a pugnacious glare at the two Chinese men and leaves. Disgruntled, Wang pushes Chang out the cell and the two men walk down the long, dark corridor as Wang continues expressing his displeasure.

The small cell is quite inadequate, and for the first time in her life, Rachel feels all alone and afraid. She glances at her watch. It's ten o'clock and there is suddenly an urgent need to remember something. She wrestles with her mind straining to remember. Nervous tension and frazzled nerves leave her weak as she wonders what it is that is trying to trigger her memory.

Rachel bows her head in her cupped hands and softly sobs... *what a pathetic mess I'm in...I don't know why I'm in this cell... I don't know if I'm in Japan or where I am...I don't know if I recognized one of my captors... and I don't know what I'm to remember at ten o'clock. I can't remember anything.*

CHAPTER FOUR

General Erik von Horstmann was frantic with worry for Rachel's safety as he paced the floor and barked questions at his lieutenant in the room.

"What do you mean she just disappeared? No one just vanishes! You were supposed to protect my daughter while she was in Hong Kong." General Von hastened to think to himself... *I never should have allowed her to handle this assignment. I knew there may be trouble... but then, that is why I assigned Adam to protect her. This is a stroke of bad luck.*

Adam reluctantly responded, "General Von, sir, I don't know how else to explain it. As you requested, I kept a respectable distance and I was vigilant in keeping a close watch on Rachel's every move. The streets by mid-morning were teeming with spectators feverishly pushing and shoving for a good advantage place to watch the celebration. One minute she was standing on the curb of the street watching the parade and the next minute she was gone."

There were a few quiet moments when nothing was said. General Von looked intently at Adam as if to study his expression, which he thought showed honest concern. He believed Adam could be trusted to execute any assignment given, competently. He had no qualm in charging Adam to guard Rachel as he was one of his most capable lieutenants. The general stood behind his desk kicking the leg of the chair with his boot, thinking... *is it possible there is someone in the compound who has betrayed me.* With his brow furrowed, the general pleaded, "Try to think, Adam. Describe the parade… and what was the last thing that happened prior to Rachel's disappearance?"

Adam began, "The parade was long, as usual, and extremely noisy and festive with many colorful floats, acrobats and musicians, etc… the typical celebration. The largest float was a huge dragon, probably thirty feet long, which was passing in front of Rachel when the whole parade stopped because of fireworks which were thrown into the procession. These were no ordinary fireworks. They were larger explosives, which excited the crowd to push back from the street. I, of course, was scanning the crowd to see if I could recognize any members of the Chinese Triad in the fracas. The Hong Kong patrol quickly apprehended a couple of coolies from the rickshaw stand, who appeared to be drunk, who were throwing the explosives and the parade continued at its slow pace. When the disturbance was over, Rachel was gone."

General Von thoughtfully surmised, "It is possible Rachel could have been whisked inside the dragon in a matter of seconds during the brief fireworks disturbance. I want you to take a couple of men with you and return to Hong Kong; find out where the wired/paper-mache dragon is stored, check it over thoroughly and report back to me."

*****

It was late in the evening when Adam returned from Hong Kong and he immediately reported to the general. "The paper-mache dragon is stored in the harbor warehouse. After a thorough search, we found an opening in the dragon where volunteers enter to manipulate its various movements. This black ribbon was inside, which Rachel was wearing in her hair to pull back her braid."

The general took the ribbon from Adam and lovingly fondled it. He struggled to hold back tears… coughed and cleared his throat to ask, "Did you return to the parade route to question anyone who may have witnessed something at that particular time when the dragon stopped?"

"Yes. I deployed the men to cover the whole distance from the starting point to where the parade ended. All shop owners along the route said they were more interested in watching the police chase the coolies who had the fireworks than they were in looking at the parade, and no one gave any attention to the dragon during that time." Adam was quick to add, "I walked to the rickshaw stand a few blocks away to talk to the coolies to see if someone could tell me the names of the coolies who were arrested." Adam stopped to light a cigarette, took a few drags and continued, "General Von, this is when the story got interesting. I was told those men were not coolies, but were members of the Triad. The coolie who gave me this information then became very nervous and did not want to continue. I told him he had better cooperate and I threw in a few threats to encourage him to talk, which he did. He hesitated a few minutes... then said that a man approached the coolie, Chang, and whispered something to him. Chang looked frightened and quickly left with the man. No one has seen Chang since that time. And the coolie, who looked scared to death if he would be seen by someone from the Triad talking to me, could not or would not give me a description of the man who took Chang."

The general acknowledged Adam's report with a nod of his head and released him to return to his duties. He wanted time alone to ponder this information. Chang had been used before as an informant when it became necessary to identify a key member of the Chinese Triad Society, and the general feared that perhaps Chang's identity had been compromised after that last caper. Possibly, he was kidnapped along with Rachel. To the general's knowledge, Chang's identity as a double agent was known only to Rachel and to one other in the compound. In deeper contemplation, the general conversely toyed with the thought that perhaps Chang was called upon by the Triad to identify Rachel in the crowd so they could achieve their goal to kidnap her. The general briefly reflected upon the last covert operation with a feeling of pride for his men who fought gallantly against the Triad... *and the Triad was defeated.* A faint smile crossed the general's face when he remembered how he out maneuvered General Tso and the Triad's conspiracy to smuggle Hitler's gold into Macau and their attempt to kidnap Rachel.

CHAPTER FIVE

The general's small house on the island of Lantau is comfortable and his office is quite adequate. There are four small dormitories on the property, which house the orphaned children, a small schoolhouse with a recreation hall, a playground and a stockade fence surrounding the entire compound, which secures it as a fortress and as a refuge for the children.

It is not a military facility. There are no barracks for personnel nor are there training grounds. It was built specifically for General Von's headquarters to serve as a police command post for planning operations against the gangs of hoodlums of the Chinese Triad Society.

When Japan invaded China in World War II, mainland China was ravaged mercilessly by the Japanese and the Chinese Triad Society offered to assist the Japanese in various criminal enterprises in many of the larger cities including Hong Kong. The members of the Society were well trained in the martial arts and violence ran rampant. These gangs of hoodlums helped police the residents of Hong Kong suppressing any anti-Japanese activity. It was estimated that there were well over one hundred thousand members in various criminal Triad gangs during that time who all worked for the Japanese. After World War II, however, there was a brief semi-dormant period of criminal activities, but the Cultural Revolution in mainland China was one of several factors that caused massive emigration and social problems causing a resurgence of these hoodlum gangs. It is this new wave of criminal activity that General Von must try to harness.

The idea of combining a police command post with an orphanage was conceived by the general's wife, Frau Horstmann. At its inception, the command post was to remain a secret entity, allowing the general and his men to plan their activities to fight gold smugglers and drug traffickers in the area. Under cover of the orphanage, the operation was successful and both the British Intelligence and the French Interpol offices were very pleased with the general's work in harnessing the violent activities of the Triad criminals. To the outside world, the compound appeared as an orphanage with no other purpose than to administer to the needs of homeless children, which idea worked for awhile. After the last confrontation with members of the Triad, the secrecy of the general's headquarters was jeopardized. The Triad is well aware of General Von's operations and they fear him as a formidable foe.

*****

Sydney arrived earlier than the other men for the meeting with General Von. There were many plans to be made and strategy to be discussed in locating Rachel and the general wanted to brief Sydney first before the others arrived.

Sydney was the general's confidant who had earned his respect after assisting in the capture of many members of the Triad in their attempt to smuggle gold in the Pearl River estuary area. Sydney was no stranger to danger. She received her training in the secret service department in Britain many years ago and was awarded three commendations for her exemplary service during the war years. Her experience included dealing with the smuggling of artifacts and gold from war-torn Germany to South America and the Orient, and her knowledge of five languages proved invaluable when it was necessary to converse with people of different nationalities.

When Sydney entered the office, the general was seated behind his desk with his head bowed in his cupped hands. His concern for Rachel was overwhelming; and when he raised his head to look at

Sydney, the deep, worried lines on his tired face showed evidence that he had not slept in two days.

"Good morning, Sydney. Please take a seat," the general requested. "I am troubled that we may have a traitor in our midst." The general emptied his coffee cup, poured another cup for himself, offered a cup to Sydney and breathing heavily continued, "Honest, loyal people are hard to find and hard to keep when a man's weak virtue consorts with an evil element that is willing to pay large sums of money for what it wants. The devil raises his ugly head to entice men to sell their soul, if need be, to gain wealth. I'm afraid we have someone here in this compound who is selling information to the Triad."

"I hope not, sir. What makes you think it is someone from this compound?" Sydney asked.

The general was slow to respond; shook his head in disbelief and wearily said, "I made certain that no one in the compound, other than you and Adam, knew that Rachel was going into Hong Kong to contact Quan Lee, the minister of narcotics; and, yet, the Triad was at the parade route ready to snatch Rachel. I questioned Adam yesterday and his first report back to me showed negligence on his part. I had to request that he return to Hong Kong to ferret out more information, which he should have done immediately following Rachel's disappearance. The crowd of celebrants had dispersed and valuable time was lost. He is one of my best lieutenants," and in a slower, lower voice he uttered, "I don't want to believe it."

Sydney sat quietly, scrutinizing the general's demeanor. He was no longer a tower of strength... a Goliath in stature. She had never seen him distressed to the point of weakness and his new persona was a little frightening. His daughter's disappearance was taking its toll and his spirit had ebbed to a new low.

"In my military career as a German officer, I had many victories... always cognizant of the number of men I lost and of the number of enemy killed. It was war and I was fighting for a justifiable cause... a glorified, new Germany. When I could no longer justify the reason for killing, I abandoned my position in the German army and was fortunate to be able to assist the allies in a coup to thwart the assassination of Churchill; and with the help of the allies, my family and I were given safe passage to Macau."

The general seemed to ramble in his speech. There was no apparent direction for his thoughts and there was silence for a few minutes. Sydney continued to sit quietly.

"When my wife was killed here at the orphanage, I felt my world crumbling. It was the three of us... my wife, Rachel and I who survived the ravages of the War and the nerve-wracking escape to the Orient. A tight bond of love, devotion and strength developed among the three of us, which was nurtured by all the narrow escapes and life-threatening ordeals. As long as we were all together, anything was possible. Now, with Rachel kidnapped, my world has collapsed."

The general sat taller in his chair and continued. "There is one redeeming factor yet in my life... and that is this orphanage. I am proud to be an instrument in the healing and safety of so many children. For me, this is my escape mechanism from my military life. I have done many things for which I am not proud and I hope God in heaven will grant me mercy for those early, ugly years."

With handkerchief in hand, the general wiped his eyes and looked squarely at Sydney, urging, "We must find Rachel and we must do it quickly! She has courage and she is strong, but I pray she will not have to endure torture. Sydney... you and Quan Lee are the only ones I feel I can trust. If you recall, Rachel was to meet with Quan Lee to give him the code numbers of the shipment of opium that is arriving in a few days. The code numbers were written on a piece of thin onion-skin paper and sewn into Rachel's black ribbon that she wore in her hair. It's ironic that Adam returned the black ribbon to me to verify that Rachel had been kidnapped. Had he only known what he held in his hand, perhaps the necessity to kidnap Rachel could have been avoided."

Sydney interrupted, "General, do you have any other evidence incriminating Adam... other than his lack of being thorough in his investigation?"

"Yes. I was late for a meeting I had scheduled with him in my office the other evening; and when I arrived, I found him moving papers on my desk. I didn't think too much about it at the time, as he said he had dropped a match on the desk after he lit his cigarette. But when he left my office, I could not find the message from Quan Lee, which stated the time and place for his meeting with Rachel in Hong Kong."

The general removed a postcard from his jacket, handed it to Sydney and said, "You, Quan Lee and I are the only ones who know that Chang occasionally works for us as a secret agent and this knowledge must be kept confidential. Here, take this. I believe this is from Chang."

Sydney looked at the card a little mystified as she read the two words scribbled on the card: Fei Hu. The card was addressed to the general and postmarked from Yokohama, Japan. "How do you know this card is from Chang?" Sydney asked.

"Do you recall Chang telling us the story of his involvement during the War with our American pilots in China, who were known as the Flying Tigers? Fei Hu is Chinese for the shark's teeth painted on their planes. Chang always referred to them as Fei Hu and he went on to explain that he learned to speak 'fine American', what we call Pidgin English, from our pilots. Adam reported that Chang was approached at the rickshaw stand by a member of the Triad, who whispered something to him, and then they both disappeared into the crowd. He has not been seen at the rickshaw stand nor has he been seen anywhere in Hong Kong since the day of the parade."

Sydney digested the general's words and with careful thought speculated, "Perhaps this is his way of telling us that he and Rachel are in Yokohama."

The card was the usual run-of-the-mill tourist postcard for mailing back home. The face of the postcard was a scenic picture of the Tokyo Bay seaport area in Yokohama, which view included some of the warehouses. "General, I believe Rachel is being held somewhere in the general vicinity of the wharf as pictured on this card. If we surmise this card is from Chang, then it appears his cover as our agent has not been blown and the Triad members still consider him to be valuable in assisting them. I would say this is a stroke of good luck."

General Von's expression brightened as he encouragingly said, "I hope so, Sydney." He continued, "I do think it strange, however, that I have not received a message from anyone taking responsibility for the abduction. I would think that General Tso would be gloating with this coup and would be eager to contact me for ransom or for whatever purpose he wishes me to grant in return for my daughter's safe return. He is a braggart who crows his accomplishments; and this one against me must be his greatest triumph. Sydney, we must not let General Tso win this one. We must rally everyone we can to help us find Rachel, quickly!"

Voices outside the general's office door alerted the general and Sydney that Quan Lee had arrived from Hong Kong along with Adam and a few other men. They entered like ducks swimming and quacking on a pond… everyone was pushing through the door and talking at the same time. The general interrupted them and asked, "What's all the excitement?"

Quan Lee was the first to speak, "This small box was handed to me before I boarded the junk in Victoria Harbor to come to Lantau." In a slow, serious tone of voice, Quan Lee continued, "This box is intended for you."

The general quickly stood up from behind the desk, met Quan Lee half way across the large room and grabbed the box from his hand. He was eager to see its contents. His large fingers nervously fumbled with the lid and he uttered a small cry as he took a gold locket from the box. He returned to the desk and flopped down in the chair… stunned.

Quan Lee continued, "General Von, sir, I was extremely careful and took every precaution to make certain I was not followed. And, yet, a young boy ran straight to me while I stood on the pier waiting to board the junk and he threw this package at me, quickly ran away and vanished in the crowd before I knew what was happening. I was his mark and he delivered the package. I don't believe he was more than seven years old."

The general stared into the box not wanting to handle its contents. It was Rachel's locket. With internalized anger, the general thought to himself... *This doesn't belong in a box! This locket belongs on Rachel's neck where it has been since her sixteenth birthday.* He opened the locket to see once again the picture of Rachel and her mother, which picture was taken shortly before her mother was killed. Everyone in the room stood quietly, respecting the general's piercing wound to his heart.

Sydney broke the silence with the request, "General, why don't we table this meeting for a couple of hours. Quan Lee and I can finish our report on opium action in Canton and the other men can return here later?"

The general flashed a quizzical look at Sydney, but acknowledged, yes, with a nod of his head.

After the other men left the room, Quan Lee produced a small piece of paper from his pocket and handed it to the general. "I didn't want the other men to see this note, which was in the box, as I'm beginning to feel paranoid that I can no longer trust anyone, so I slipped it into my pocket."

The note was signed by General Tso and briefly stated his demand for unbridled control for his drug trafficking activities. In return, he would release Rachel unharmed.

General Von said, "General Tso knows we have made plans to confiscate the large shipment of opium leaving Canton in a few weeks, which explains this second attempt to kidnap Rachel. The Triad knew that she was carrying a note to be delivered to you that had all the pertinent information regarding the drug seizure. Quan Lee, you'll be happy to hear the note did not fall into General Tso's hands when she was kidnapped. By a stroke of good luck, the note was retrieved along with her black hair ribbon, as the note was sewn in the ribbon's seam.

"And I have more news, Quan Lee. Take a look at this postcard."

Quan Lee smiled, "It's a note from Chang, right? I heard all about Rachel's kidnapping and Chang's involvement at the parade."

General Von interjected, "You know, Quan Lee, we have someone in our group who is selling information to the Triad… and Sydney and I think it is Adam."

Sydney was quick to add, "I watched Adam very closely when you opened the box and removed the locket. He stretched his neck to see deeper into the box as if he were expecting something else to be produced. He looked surprised when there was nothing else in the box. I definitely think he is our man."

"Yes, I believe he is," the general acknowledged. "We are going to have to decide how we want to handle this situation. Nothing should be done until after we have rescued Rachel." With a strong, determined voice he added, "And we will rescue her! And we will use Adam to our advantage in planning our strategy." He continued with the caveat, "If General Tso thinks he can threaten me by holding my daughter hostage, he had better think again. That bastard hasn't experienced my full wrath and I will make him regret the day he planned this personal attack."

The general paced the floor contemplating his next move while Sydney and Quan Lee worked at the conference table on the Canton drug report. He stopped his stride abruptly, turned to the two at the table and said, "I understand the children are asking for Rachel. I think it is best that I talk to them to ease their concern."

*****

A cold, blustery wind whipped across the orphanage compound on Lantau while snow showers drenched the island into a muddy sea of puddles. The already depressed atmosphere at the orphanage was intensified by the wet, dismal day. The orphaned children and teachers gathered in the recreation hall at the request of General Von. They did not know what to expect, but assumed the general's message would have something to do with Rachel's not returning to the compound. All the children loved Rachel, whom they considered to be their guardian angel as she filled their days with happiness. She helped them to forget the misery of their prior existence, where daily experiences involved life-threatening situations in their war-torn country. The lost and abandoned children came seeking asylum and found a haven of safety and love at the orphanage.

Several teachers had heard rumors from some of the men in the compound that Rachel was kidnapped while in Hong Kong. The general was greatly disturbed upon hearing this and quickly dispatched orders to his men that Rachel's disappearance was not to be discussed. Teachers were not privy to any of the police activities which were planned on the compound, as the general insisted upon secrecy in the performance of police operations, and he became sorely agitated when the rumor evolved. He did not want the story to be falsified and distorted in any way where it could become a portent of an evil situation.

There was absolutely no laughter nor noise of any kind in the recreation hall as over one hundred orphans sat quietly waiting for General Von. The general was not a tall man, rather paunchy, and the children liked to refer to him as Grandfather Von. He was a man bearing dual personalities: his military reputation was one of valor and courage, being bold-spirited with pluck and tenacity; and the children loved him for being gentle and kind-hearted.

He entered the hall carrying a swagger stick, which in fact was a riding crop. By no means does it show an affected mannerism for he has earned the right to this foible by having served in the German cavalry in World War I, and continued to carry the crop when he commanded an armored tank division in World War II. It has become his lucky charm. The ever-present riding crop has accompanied him during many difficult situations.

The general stood before the children for a few quiet seconds before speaking. He slowly scanned the room, looking at all the concerned facial expressions, even on the smaller children, and he realized for the first time how very proud he is of all these orphans. They have become his extended family. They have all experienced tragedy in their short life, enduring pain that may live with them forever. Now, they are building a new life under his protection and he feels a strong commitment to the memory of his wife to maintain the orphanage environment at a high level of security… where happiness abounds. He does not want to say anything that may bring fear back into their life and he starts to speak: "I've asked you to come to this assembly this morning so I can quell any fear you may have regarding Rachel. Some have mentioned she may have been kidnapped while in Hong Kong. This is not true! Rachel and I discussed her visiting a few friends in Macau before she returns home… and that is what she has done. I don't want to see any long, sad faces. You'll see. She will be back."

The recreation hall was still extremely quiet. No one moved. The general was not certain if the children believed him. They had become accustomed to disappointment and did not give way to happiness freely. He ventured upon an idea, which would include their help in bringing Rachel home and he asked, "I want us all to bow our heads and say a short prayer that Rachel will return home safely in a few days."

After the general's short message, the sun broke through the clouds causing sunlight to stream through the large windows in the recreation hall. The bright, golden light grabbed the children's attention as they turned to look and they believed it to be a good omen. The children knew that if anyone could work a miracle, if one were required, it would be Grandfather Von.

CHAPTER SIX

"I sure got a kick out of Emily's letter." Ian chuckled to Seth. "The newspapers at home are giving the impression that the South Koreans are the only ones doing any fighting, which she says eases her mind that we are not in the 'thick of things'. Can you believe that?" Ian asked Seth, but not wanting an answer. "Someone should educate those journalists as to what is going on over here. The South Koreans can't be trusted. They are ill-trained, poorly equipped and lack discipline. They bugout when the fighting gets tough and leave our troops stranded. Just the other night the South Koreans' 9th R.O.K. outfit pulled off the line and left a big gap through which the Chinese poured. Luckily our 245th tank outfit moved into the area along with our infantry and pushed the Reds back. I certainly hope the South Koreans become better soldiers soon… believe me, I don't like our troops fighting alone."

Nothing was said for quite a few minutes as both Ian and Seth sadly thought about the horrendous, bloody skirmish the night before when so many men were killed. Whatever the hometown papers say, they both know they are fighting soldiers on the front line and 'in the thick of things'. Ian added, "Well, Seth, maybe it's better if the folks at home don't know everything that's going on here. I'm sure they're plenty worried about us."

"Have you heard the news?" Seth asked. "Our unit has been ordered to fall back about four or five miles from our main line of resistance to a reserved area. We are being replaced by the 40th Infantry Division, and Major Tamermia has requested that I assist him again in his office." Seth chuckled, "I learned early in basic training not to volunteer for anything; but my hand would go up fast when they needed a typist, and being able to type has rescued me from a lot of tough, ugly duties. Volunteering to be a clerk typist for Major Tamermia is the smartest thing I've done so far in the army. I've got to admit… the job has its perks. It sure beats cleaning machine-gun barrels. And to think the only reason I signed up for typing in high school was to have a class with my girlfriend."

"Oh, gee," Ian joylessly said, "I was hoping we would go back much farther. We'll still be able to hear bed-check Charlie flying over the hillsides at ten o'clock. The crackled drone of the engine in that old one-prop plane keeps reminding me of where I am." He facetiously added, "Harassment or not, though, after that Red pilot drops his load of bombs, I know I can fall asleep. So I guess it's like counting sheep. He drops his hand-held bombs and then that's it… and I'm asleep."

Seth added, "Well, I for one will be happy to have a break from this fighting area," and sarcastically continued, "Who knows, maybe it's true about what the South Koreans call their country…'the land of the morning calm'. Maybe we can find peace and happiness farther south." Both men laughed.

*****

Standing six feet four inches, weighing two hundred twenty pounds and exceedingly handsome, Major Tamermia cuts quite a figure in his uniform. He is embarrassed to remember that when he enlisted to serve in World War II, his picture was on posters to recruit young men into the army. Of course, the poster of Uncle Sam pointing his finger and saying, "I want you" was also predominantly displayed and the two posters together caught the attention of many young men. The men under his command respectfully refer to him as the "ol' man" as he is thirty-six years old, fought in World War II and awarded two medals in the European campaign: The Silver Star and the Distinguished Service Cross. He is a professional soldier. His deep voice resounds with clarity and authority and it is his knowledge of tactical experience that has earned him the confidence of his men. Major Tamermia is an army intelligence officer, and when recalled to a rear position, he is the division prosecuting attorney handling special courts-martial cases. It is during this time that he asks Seth to assist him in writing and typing case briefs.

The headquarters tent is fairly large, accommodating a few tables, chairs, portable typewriter, maps of the area and everything needed to command from that location. The battalion commanding officer, Lieutenant Colonel Pritchard, is the highest ranking officer and Seth, a corporal, is the lowest ranking non-commissioned officer. Everything in the tent is portable allowing for a fast pack-and-run if necessary.

*****

Daylight hours pass quickly for Seth. His duties are demanding of his skill in assisting the major and he appreciates always being able to work in a dry, fairly warm tent. It is the night hours that drag on from one distressing hour filled with anxiety for Rachel's safety to many hours depriving him of sleep, which cause him mental anguish. His heart aches with worry. The same questions keep pounding in his head. *Why haven't I received a letter? Has she been caught in some cloak-and-dagger spy game plan? Has she forgotten me? Does she no longer love me?*

Seth is a romantic who enjoys conjuring up daydreams of mystical vignettes that are pleasing to his intellectual liking. When he was in college studying to be an architect, his dreams were to design beautiful buildings that would be admired by others... a legacy to the world, which he hopes some day to fulfill. His immediate dreams reflect his love for Rachel and his deep concern for her safety. He likes to linger longer upon one particular recurring dream where he wishes time could stand still when he can forget for a few moments his present dangerous situation as a soldier in Korea and dream of Rachel. His emotions become stimulated by his thoughts of the first time he kissed Rachel. He relives the excitement of holding her tenderly in his arms... feeling the warmth of her curvaceous body pressed against his and the responsive touch of her lips. After the long kiss, he watched her beautiful eyes slowly open to look up into his and he knew he had succumbed to her sensual appeal. A spell was cast that overpowered all his emotions and he knew he was in love.

Major Tamermia stops Seth's reverie with the question: "You look like you're a thousand miles away?"

"Yes, sir, I was. I haven't received a letter from my girlfriend for quite awhile and I hope she hasn't forgotten me. We had a whirlwind romance shortly before I was drafted and sent over here. I'm worried she may send me a 'Dear John' letter."

"Hey, corporal, stop worrying," the major said encouragingly. "No young girl could forget a good looking guy like you. I'm certain everything is okay."

The major turned to look for a file on his desk when he remembered Seth was in the process of typing the case brief and asked, "Corporal do you have Private Wilson's brief typed, yet? I need it pretty quickly."

"Sorry, sir. I'll have it finished in a minute."

The major became pensive with a thought and suggested to Seth, "Tonight, why don't you and a buddy take a walk to division headquarters. It's down the road about a mile or so to the campsite where, I understand, the men have put up a Quonset hut to show movies. It may do you some good. I hear the movie tonight is 'Singin' in the Rain' with Gene Kelly, Donald O'Connor and Debbie Reynolds. Now, there's real talent for you. I bet it's going to be good."

"Thank you, sir," Seth cheerfully responded. "That sounds like a great idea!"

*****

The night air was cold and crisp with a full moon flooding its brilliant light over the snow-covered deep ruts of the frozen mud road. Seth and Ian chuckled over the signs posted along the way for military halftracks to "make your own rut"; and for the two soldiers… walking was difficult. But they knew if they ventured too far from the side of the road, there was the fear of stepping on a land mine.

With their rifles slung over their shoulder with the muzzle pointing down to the ground, both soldiers wore a poncho, which kept them fairly warm. They did not wear the iron pot on their head... only the helmet liner, but it was the pocket warmers that helped to make the long trek more bearable. They passed many checkpoints along the way to division headquarters. At each checkpoint a guard called out, "Halt! Who goes there?" Seth answered the password for the evening, which was "tommy", and the guard answered, "gun" and passed the soldiers on their way.

The crunch of snow beneath their boots was the only sound to break the silence as the two men trudged the long road. Ian tried several times to initiate a conversation, but Seth was content to remain quiet in a melancholy mood and answered only sporadically. Ian's temperament was of a lighter spirit and he wanted to enjoy the evening... his first evening away from camp. He wanted to try to forget the war, if only for a few hours, and to block out the ever-present sound of shells exploding in the distance, which was a constant reminder that somewhere close by there was a battle raging and men were dying. Again, he split the silence and broached the question, "I've noticed Major Tamermia has kind of taken you under his wing. I think he likes you. What do you think?"

Seth replied, "The major says I remind him of his kid brother, whom he helped raise." With a tone of admiration he continued, "The longer I work with him, the more I admire his quick sense of jurisprudence. He knows the law and his decisions are fair. I feel proud to be a small cog in the wheel in his courtroom."

Ian jokingly added, "That's quite a testimonial."

With a serious, low voice Seth stopped Ian and forcibly said, "If ever circumstances should demand it on the battlefield, I'd follow him to the gates of hell."

Ian wanted to change Seth's solemn mood and quipped, "Well, let's all hope we won't have to go that far in this bloody war."

Ian finally gave up the idea of lifting Seth's spirits and decided to walk quietly along side.

Seth was absorbed in his own thoughts. The cold night air reminded him of the many winter nights when he and his Cider Club friends would ice skate on one of the many lakes close to home. The young boys would enjoy warming their cold feet beside a campfire and would weave adventurous tales of daring deeds they had experienced playing on the Ramsey plantation. The stories always involved the large vacant mansion where the local neighbors believed the ghost of old man Ramsey walked the halls. The toughest dare to accept was to spend one night alone in the stately mansion, which was mandatory if any boy wanted to join the Cider Club. This was a time when childhood friendships blossomed… when boys had grandiose ideas of becoming famous, carving a successful career, making the world a better place in which to live. A few of these boys were drafted into World War II and they all died in the European campaign. Seth is the first of the remaining Cider Club members to be drafted into the Korean War. His thoughts stray to his wondering if he will return home safely… or…. Seth realized he was becoming too maudlin. He is a dreamer, but he did not like the direction this dream was taking him.

"I was just thinking about some of the crazy things I used to do when I was a kid growing up on a large plantation. What games do you remember playing as a kid?" Seth asked.

Ian was happy to hear the question and eagerly answered, "Well, I grew up in Oklahoma among the oil wells. Not that my dad owned any, but he worked on the oil rigs and he was plenty good at it, too." Ian said with pride. "We played cowboys and Indians a lot," and he continued more light heartedly, "That really wasn't too much fun for me, though. When the guys asked me to be one of the Cherokee Indians, I always knew we were supposed to lose. That's the way the game had to end. The rich kids always got to be the cowboys."

Both men stepped up their pace faster as the cold wind started to blow through the valley with more intensity. A few lights from division headquarters sparkled in the night sky indicating the Quonset hut was a short distance ahead.

*****

The moon, now on the wane, continued to cast its light on the long road. Bright stars twinkled, the wind blew the snow into deep drifts, and the two soldiers left the Quonset hut taking long strides in a brisk walk. Their attitude on the return journey was extremely different. Both men took turns recalling various hilarious scenes from the movie and repeated many times the silly dialogue, which brought uproarious laughter from the soldiers in the Quonset hut. The movie had served its purpose. The soldiers had immersed themselves into another world where there was joy and laughter. The road back to camp seemed shorter as there were no spells of silence... Seth and Ian rambled on in a happy chatter.

Seth suddenly called, "Look, Ian! There's a falling star. Quick! Make a wish!"

Seth's wish came to him very quickly... before the star faded from view. Both men became quiet as they silently made their wish. Seth reverently thought, which was a prayer rather than a wish... *Please, let me hear from Rachel...and have her love me always.*

Seth believed the weight of the world had been lifted from his shoulders. He felt an inner calm, which relaxed his tension, and said, "Ian, that falling star is a sign of good luck."

CHAPTER SEVEN

General Von, Sydney and Quan Lee sat late into the afternoon hours pouring over a hodgepodge of maps of the harbor area in Yokohama, Japan, replete with plans of the warehouse district along the wharf, which were spread before them on the huge table in the general's office. The scenic postcard of the seaport area, which they received from Chang and which they presumed to be a clue as to where Rachel is being held captive, rested against the lamp on the general's desk. The three sat silently at the table with blank stares as the long meeting had produced no viable plan for Rachel's rescue from her abductors.

General Von broke the silence and in a low, dejected tone uttered, "We could sit here until hell freezes studying these papers." In an angry loud voice he continued, "We don't know for certain that this postcard is from Chang; and if it is, which room in which warehouse is now Rachel's cell? We can't storm them all… which is what I would like to do." He continued, "Our men have found no clues, which could lead us to Rachel…" the general's voice trailed off, "we only know that General Tso has my daughter and we have only a few weeks to find her."

Sydney watched the general in disbelief. His countenance no longer exuded the confidence of a general who had commanded thousands of soldiers. He is now a father who is expressing deep concern for his daughter.

The general continued venting his anger while pacing the floor and nervously swishing his riding crop back and forth. With a mournful sigh, he flopped into his chair.

"Please excuse my outburst. My emotions are too frazzled to use realistic thought in making any formidable plans. I'm too close to this one. I want to rush somewhere to rescue my daughter and I don't even know where she is."

The long futile hours of the afternoon wore on, and the sun slowly disappeared from the winter sky. The hours waned into evening, prompting the dimming light through the windows to shroud the office with a blanket of somberness. When the general reached to turn on the lamp at his desk to bring light into the room, he knocked the postcard from the desk to the floor. He retrieved the card and again placed it at the base of the lamp. The bright light fell across the scenic view of the warehouses. The general felt dazed with worry and continued staring at the card. After a few seconds, he jumped to his feet and with a burst of enthusiasm, yelled, "Merciful heaven! Sydney, Quan Lee, come… look at the card under this light!"

Both Sydney and Quan Lee jumped to their feet and rushed to the desk… their eyes became transfixed on the postcard.

"What? What do you see?" Sydney questioned.

"Look closely at the many windows of the warehouses. Do you see it?" the general asked.

Quan Lee murmured, "I don't see anything unusual."

Sydney picked up the card and held it closer to her eyes and directly under the bright light. "I see it!" she cried. "Look, Quan Lee, this window has a curtain drawn on it in blue ink."

"My goodness! What eyes you have. Yes, I see the tiny blue lines, which are topical for certain and are not printed into the card."

"Yes! Yes! That's it. Chang is telling us that this is the room in the warehouse where Rachel is being held."

The general vigorously rubbed his hands together and joyfully said, "Now, we can make some real plans."

*****

The three sat for an hour hurling ideas across the table in an urgent need to come up with a good plan.

"Quan Lee, I have concerns with your suggestion to use mercenary soldiers in extricating Rachel from her abductors. I know we used a few, and I might add to good advantage, in capturing the gold smugglers in Macau a year ago, but my daughter's rescue is going to take us to Yokohama and I don't want to take mercenary soldiers into Japan. In fact, I think we should use only a few men for the rescue," the general proposed.

"Perhaps you're right." Quan Lee yielded, but with the caveat, "We must choose our men carefully." With a cautious tone of voice, he continued, "I don't want to use any of my policemen from Hong Kong, as I am certain most of them are well known by members of the Triad, and I think…"

The general picked up the sentence from there and added, "I think three or four men should be all that will be needed, and I don't want to use anyone from this command post, either. I don't know who I can trust."

Both, the general and Quan Lee, agreed the men selected should be knowledgeable in the use of weapons, able to speak in Chinese and Japanese and capable of defending themselves under difficult situations.

"Stay here." The general called to Quan Lee and Sydney as he ran out the door. "I think I have an idea."

Quan Lee and Sydney placed the postcard on the spate of maps before them on the table. They were quick to locate the exact warehouse; and after a thorough study of the blueprints, they isolated the very room that was indicated on the card, presumably, to be Rachel's cell. They felt charged with excitement and intoxicated with joy. Both expressed their ideas for Rachel's rescue at the same time in a hurried manner… neither one hearing the other's idea when the general returned… talking as he entered the room.

"I remember watching Rachel tenderly fondle some letters, which she tied with a blue ribbon and placed in the drawer of her nightstand at the side of her bed. I know these letters are from Seth, who was drafted into the army and is now stationed in Korea. And I think I have a plan. Now, hear me out.

"Sydney, I know you remember Seth as you both sailed to Hong Kong aboard the tramp steamer, *Ladybug*."

"Oh, I remember that young man very well. Who could forget such a handsome young man… tall and built like an Adonis with beautiful eyes and…"

The general interrupted at this point, chuckled and said, "Well, Sydney, it seems you were quite taken with Seth. Come to think of it, I guess he does have all those attributes. I just didn't pay much attention at the time."

Quan Lee added, "Yes, I remember him, also. He acquitted himself in a fine manner and showed great courage when we fought against the Triad in their attempt to kidnap Rachel and confiscate the gold from the *Ladybug* in Macau."

Quan Lee and Sydney were anxious to hear the plan and listened intently with mental faculties that were sharp and eager to grasp the general's strategy.

The general continued, "Rachel mentioned to me that in her last letter she received from Seth, he stated he will be eligible for R-and-R in the next few weeks and he will be sent to Japan for a few days. She asked me if I thought she could get away from the orphanage for awhile to join Seth in Japan." The general paused at this point with a fatherly thought… *Rachel must really like this young man. Perhaps, as a father, I've been negligent in certain matters and remiss to Rachel's feelings.* With a shake of his head as if to reprimand himself, he continued, "Instead of rest and recuperation, I think Seth is our man to rescue Rachel."

Quan Lee was quick to add, "Seth is well trained in marital arts; and with his military training, he may be the man we need to rescue Rachel;" then dishearteningly Quan Lee continued, "but he doesn't understand Chinese or Japanese."

With an air of confidence for his plan, and directing his remark to Sydney, the general stated, "I think you should go also since you understand and speak both languages… plus you and Seth know Chang."

The general was exhilarated when he continued, "It will be up to me to get the army to allow Seth to take his R-and-R in Japan right away, as speed of deployment to this operation is urgent. My contacts in the Pentagon in Washington, D.C. are quite reliable and I know they will do this for me." And to himself he thought: *They owe me at least one favor for my part in post-war intelligence surveillance of drug trafficking and gold smuggling in the Orient.*

The three looked from one to the other with big smiles on their face, shaking their head thinking... *yes, this is a good plan.*

The excitement generated by the three was comparable to an electric charge igniting a light to shine through the darkness. The general's idea had burst forth with a ray of hope for Rachel's rescue.

CHAPTER EIGHT

Quan Lee's greatest adversary in the performance of his duties as minister of Hong Kong Security Division and Narcotics Control in the twenty-mile wide Pearl River estuary area of Hong Kong, Macau and Canton is his childhood friend, Yen Tso. Both boys were born to uneducated, indigent families on the south side of Hong Kong Island. Their fathers were life-long friends who depended upon each other in their daily hard-earned effort as fishermen to support their families. They lived on unwieldy junks in the floating city of Aberdeen Harbor that was a fishing village built on the water, which was home to over twenty thousand people who lived on houseboats. Small sampans shuttled across the bay to a plethora of haphazardly constructed buildings, which lined the harbor's banks creating a soulful scene of a shantytown. Many times, the boys accompanied their fathers to the Tin Hau Temple where they burned incense to the Queen of Heaven and the Protectress of Seafarers worshipping the fishermen's guardian spirit.

Quan Lee and Yen were raised as if they were blood brothers, learning the arduous trade of commercial fishing from their fathers. Unlike their fathers, the boys were permitted to attend school. Playtime was rare, but once in awhile they would sneak away to play hide-and-seek among the headstones in the old Chinese Permanent Cemetery, which was built on the hillside overlooking Aberdeen Bay. This was a special hideout for the boys where they had the freedom to create games exemplifying honor and valor in fighting off the hordes of Mongols invading their small world of Aberdeen. They shared ideas and dreams, which always included living somewhere else other than on a junk in Aberdeen Bay. They both shared the same dream to be buried with their ancestors in the Permanent Cemetery. This was an honor as the body would never be exhumed for cremation, which is the practice in China after six months interment. The outside world was ravished with social, political and economic chaos at this time, but as small boys they knew nothing of the larger world beyond Aberdeen.

When the Japanese invaded China a few years later, both were eager to leave Aberdeen and their Spartan life. On Christmas Day, 1941, the island of Hong Kong, the Gibraltar of the Orient, crumbled under a massive invasion of Japanese troops. Quan Lee and Yen were among the first young men eager to embark upon a journey that would carry them far from Aberdeen. Their career paths separated them, however, eventually taking them in different directions.

Yen joined the army and had a brilliant military career. He proved to have indomitable courage leading his men in many successful campaigns against the Japanese. Promotions came quickly and soon all of China knew him as the most honorable General Tso. Quan Lee enjoyed reading about his friend's achievements and was proud to think of him as his brother. After the War, General Yen Tso used his military experience to become the leader of one of the strongest evil Triad groups in the triangular peninsula of the Pearl River delta, which is the hotbed area for opium and gold smuggling. It is now well know by the Hong Kong authorities that General Tso's base of operation is in Panama where he has complete control of operations in the Orient, as well as in the Middle East.

Quan Lee's military career was not as illustrious. He was not as fortunate as Yen to leave the Hong Kong area. His tour of duty was spent in Hong Kong working undercover fighting the gangsters of the Triad societies that ran criminal enterprises for the Japanese. These gangs were united by the Japanese in Hong Kong under an association called the Hing Ah Kee Kwan, and were used to help police the residents of Hong Kong and to suppress any anti-Japanese activity. They were paid by the Japanese. It was a few years after the War when Mao Tse Tung's communists emerged as victors that the Triad nationalists were dispersed in Hong Kong and Macau. To a large degree, this was due to Quan Lee's ability to ferret out and arrest thousands of suspected mobsters. There were countless Triad groups that existed; but after this cleansing, the gangs went into a semi-dormant period.

After Quan Lee was released from military service, he was retained by the Hong Kong authorities to continue his work in fighting the Triad gangs, which were again resurfacing. It is to his embarrassment and humiliation when he remembers that his childhood friend, Yen Tso, is now leading one of the strongest evil Triad groups. Quan Lee becomes livid with anger when his thoughts succumb to brotherly concerns for Yen while reminiscing about their childhood days in Aberdeen… thoughts that strike a sympathetic resonance that lie deeply within him. He reprimands himself for having any lingering brotherly feelings for Yen, whose dastardly deeds bring great shame and dishonor to his father. In the last three years, an abyss of hatred has deepened between the two, and brotherly love no longer exists. Quan Lee is vigilant in his determination to subdue these criminal gangs and he is becoming impatient to capture General Tso.

There is one hurdle that must be broached before meetings continue with General Von and Sydney regarding plans to free Rachel from her captor, General Tso. Quan Lee is now convinced that he has no choice other than to tell General Von that he and Yen Tso were childhood friends. To reveal this information, which he has carefully guarded for many years, will bring dishonor to his family, but he has no recourse. It is in the best interest of planning Rachel's capture that he reveals this information to General Von.

CHAPTER NINE

A waxing moon showered the compound with ribbons of soft light bouncing between the floating clouds. Everything in General Von's office appeared brighter, also, as General Von, Sydney and Quan Lee were now rejuvenated in their planning process after determining the location of the room in the warehouse where Rachel is being held captive. The atmosphere definitely took a turn for the better. Quan Lee felt it was time to tell his story and he told it with alacrity… eager at first to divulge his childhood memories of Aberdeen and the many youthful experiences that united the two boys in a brotherly bond. He continued speaking fondly of Yen during the early years of the War with no hesitation of his accomplishments.

As he unraveled Yen's life after the War years, General Von and Sydney listened intently and noticed a transformation in Quan Lee's countenance where his whole demeanor changed to a look of hostility and his words became bitter. Quan Lee expressed with deep regret the drastic change of valued character traits which overpowered Yen. Quan Lee explained it was a metamorphosis that had besieged him… as if an evil spirit had swallowed him and then spit him out completely transformed into a man with no honor, loyalty or virtues.

At this moment in the story, Quan Lee had convinced himself that Yen had been reborn to answer only to the evil spirits with their vile, despicable behavior. Quan Lee rationalized this was the only answer to his drastically changed behavior. He believed it was justified that family ties between Yen and his father had long been severed and that Yen's name was never again mentioned in the Aberdeen fishing village.

A great silence fell upon the room and the three sat staring into space... Quan Lee burdened with a shackle of remorse, Sydney feeling Quan Lee's pain, and General Von contemplating how he can use this information to the best advantage for Rachel's rescue.

General Von's mind was racing with options now available in Rachel's capture: he knows the exact location where she is being held; he feels certain he can obtain a military release for Seth to initiate a rest and recuperation period for him for a few days in Japan to assist in Rachel's capture; he knows Sydney will be extremely vital in Rachel's rescue as she is fluent in both Chinese and Japanese; he knows Quan Lee's extensive personal knowledge of Yen Tso's character traits and military maneuvers will prove invaluable; and he has decided to take an active part in the rescue of his daughter. He does not discount the assistance he will receive from Chang once they are able to make contact with him. He realizes Chang is in a very dangerous, precarious situation, being an operative for both sides, as a double agent's life always hangs in the balance during a crucial encounter... and he will use Chang with caution. He also remembers Adam, one of his own lieutenants, whose lust for money has corrupted his morality motivating him to sell information to the enemy. He is not to be trusted.

The large hall clock chimed six breaking the silence, reminding General Von of the dinner hour. He quickly jumped to his feet, grabbed his riding crop and said in a lively, rejuvenated tone of voice, "Come! Let's join the children for dinner. They always like it when I am present in their dining hall. I think they feel more secure when they see me occasionally."

Sydney was quick to stand and enthusiastically said, "Yes, let's get something to eat. I'm starving."

Quan Lee sat for a few seconds... then quietly murmured, "Yes, that sounds like a good idea. I'm hungry, too."

As the three left the office, General Von took precaution to lock his office door as he did not want any of his men to see the blueprints, which were scattered on his desk. He believed only Quan Lee and Sydney should be privy to any strategic plans that are being made.

*****

The dining hall was bustling with children scurrying to sit at a table close to Grandfather Von, who after prayers and dinner, would tell them a wonderful fairy tale. Most of the time he would tell children's stories, which are written by Hans Christian Andersen and were Rachel's favorite when she was a little girl. They especially liked the story "The Emperor's New Clothes" and Grandfather Von could always get the smaller children to giggle as he would embellish upon the Emperor's whimsical shenanigans. He became the orphans' Pied Piper and they gravitated to his kindness, which he liberally expressed. There was always a flurry of excitement when he dined with the children.

Sydney and Quan Lee were quick to notice the general's deportment of a gentler manner and an outward affection for the orphans. The tired, harsh facial lines, which were easily evident when he sat in his office brooding over what plans to execute regarding Rachel's capture, had now succumbed to a softer, more relaxed demeanor. As he pulled out a chair to sit down, his eyes scanned the dining hall, looking from one table of happy faces to another and he was proud to have a significant role in supporting the orphanage.

He gently spoke, "Daily, we deal with problems regarding drug trafficking and gold smuggling… and we speak only of the ugly people in Hong Kong and Macau. We must not forget the many fine people in China who are kind and considerate; who are willing to put their lives at risk to rid their country of the scum who feast like vultures on their own kind. Our mission work and especially the orphanage we maintain have put us in contact with so many wonderful people on this island of Lantau. The men assist with construction of additional buildings when needed and the women make clothes for our children. These are all poor people, but they are willing to sacrifice and share what they have. And the monks from the Po Lin Monastery are generous beyond belief. They provide milk for our many orphaned children who grow to adults here… and one-by-one move out to pursue their place in the world. This is what makes the dark side of my life all worthwhile." General Von's voice grew stronger and he forcefully continued, "I want these children to grow up in a healthy environment and to have the opportunity to live in a society where the evil element has been harnessed."

The general vigorously rubbed his hands through his hair in a gesture of frustration and urged, "We must not let men like General Yen Tso win."

CHAPTER TEN

Once General Von felt assured he knew where Rachel was being held captive in Japan, his actions were swift and plans were quickly formulated for stationing his people in strategic locations in the Tokyo/Yokohama area. The first order of business was to contact the Pentagon in Washington, D. C. to obtain Seth's release from Korea. He thoroughly outlined the urgency of his request for Seth's rest and recuperation furlough to Japan, and he was exceedingly pleased when the Pentagon quickly responded affirmatively to his request.

He thought it best that Quan Lee and Sydney travel separately to Japan to avoid suspicion. Quan Lee booked the first flight out of Hong Kong for Yokohama charged with instructions that he was to locate Chang in Chinatown, but he was not to make contact. Quan Lee was familiar with the Chinese district as he had visited his cousin many times in Japan, and he felt he would have no trouble in finding Chang quickly, as he presumed he would be a rickshaw coolie in Chinatown as he had been a coolie in Hong Kong.

Sydney followed immediately on the next flight out of Hong Kong to fly to Tokyo where she would masquerade as a nurse in the army hospital. Her task was to be the direct contact to talk to Chang after he was located.

*****

Quan Lee enjoyed visiting his cousin, who owned a small meat market in Chinatown, Yokohama. His visits were always for a couple of days, while he attended security meetings, conducting seminars on the newest methods of handling Chinese criminals in Chinatown and returning them to Hong Kong for incarceration. He was looking forward to this visit expecting to have more time to talk to his cousin and reminisce about family gatherings in the "old" days. Quan Lee's temperament leaned toward the nostalgia, often times becoming melancholy when thinking about his ancestors and life in general in the fishing village of Aberdeen where living was an every day hardship. His loyalty and love for family was ingrained at an early age establishing his devoted genetic characteristics. Quan Lee was a man you could count on when needed. It was easy to understand why General Von selected Quan Lee to assist in capturing Rachel. Once friendship was established, his loyalty knew no bounds.

Quan Lee had already scoped out Chang's location at the rickshaw stand in Chinatown and had given this information to Sydney, who was stationed in the army hospital in Tokyo. Sydney was to be the direct contact with Chang.

Before General Von left his headquarters on Lantau for Canton, he placed a call to the army hospital in Tokyo to verify that plans, which were previously made with the hospital authorities, were in effect for Sydney to work at the hospital. General Von's phone conversation with Sydney was short as he did not want anyone to monitor the call from his field of operation. He trusted no one at headquarters.

"Are you comfortable with your position in the hospital?" The general questioned.

"Yes. The chief administrator has placed me at the receptionist's desk in the lobby, which gives me unrestricted use of the phone and an opportunity to talk with anyone who approaches the desk. I think this will work better than masquerading as a nurse." Sydney responded.

The general was quick to add, "I have been notified that Seth is flying from Seoul, South Korea, tomorrow for Yokota Air Force Base in Japan and I have notified the colonel to call you immediately upon Seth's arrival for further instructions. Have you been able to contact Chang in Chinatown?"

"Oh, yes! Quan Lee was quick to discover where Chang lives while working as a coolie in Chinatown and I had no trouble in contacting him," Sydney enthusiastically reported. "I will not leave the receptionist's desk tomorrow for anything until I hear from the colonel regarding Seth's arrival time."

"Sydney, I am leaving for Canton and I am taking Adam with me." The general lamented, "I hope I can come up with an ingenious plan to rescue Rachel once I am in Canton." With a brighter tone in his voice, the general continued, "We have the element of surprise on our side. General Tso does not know we will be waiting for him in Japan when he arrives from Panama." With more enthusiasm and a higher pitched voice, he exclaimed, "And we know in which warehouse Rachel is being held captive."

Sydney strongly asserted, "I have a good feeling about this operation, sir."

*****

General Von knew he would have to delay his trip to Japan until he could reconcile proper handling of the Canton drug smuggling caper where General Tso's Triad hoodlums were planning to transport a large shipment of opium from Canton to Panama. General Von vividly recalled that General Tso's ransom note specified that no harm would come to Rachel if no one interfered with the shipment of opium. He knew he would have to travel to Canton to command this operation personally, and he emphatically thought… *there will be no mistakes made in Canton that will jeopardize Rachel's capture and I'll personally see to that!*

The one man General Von could not trust in this operation was Adam, and he knew he had to keep a close watch on his every move. He decided to take Adam with him on the short distance up the Pearl River to Canton.

General Von struggled with multiple ideas that spun around in his head. He experienced strong ambivalent feelings which he had fought every day since Rachel's kidnapping. He strived to be rational in making plans to capture her, realizing he had to harness his energetic desire to rush fool-heartedly to Japan, storm the warehouse by force, and take his daughter.

His troubled thoughts involved his capability to shape a deceptive plan to confuse Adam. A plan whereby Adam would be made to believe the shipment of opium from Canton to Panama would take place on schedule with no interference. And, yet, the plan must bring to fruition a successful rescue operation to free Rachel.

He also wrestled with frustrating inherent emotions of his driving desire to leave immediately for Japan to rescue his daughter and to forget about Canton altogether. That course of action, however, would be contrary to his moral, professional obligations, and that would not be possible. He believed his course of action could be better planned if he were in Canton, where he hoped to reconnoiter and study what action he should take in thwarting the drug smuggling to Panama, and still be able to save Rachel from her captors. There were serious decisions to be made. His head hurt from trying to concoct a successful plan of action that would appease Adam in thinking the opium shipment would be unabated. He felt angry, frustrated and helpless. None of his plans qualified as being worthy to assure his daughter's safe release from her captors. Dejected and filled with remorse, he blamed himself for Rachel's kidnapping. He should never have allowed her to become involved in his dangerous work.

General Von sat quietly alone in his dark office. He spun in his chair to look out the window at the star-filled heaven. The moon cast a silvery beam of light from heaven that fell brightly on the window of Rachel's bedroom. On occasion, he liked to dabble with the concept of mental telepathy, where he could become clairvoyant and transfer his thoughts to another. There were times during the War when he believed he had extrasensory perception, took advantage of it, and more than once led his troops to a successful victory. He hoped that he would be blessed again with the sixth sense in extricating his daughter from Japan. He continued to stare at the beam of light upon her window, making a concentrated effort to think only of Rachel. Tears filled his eyes as he reverently issued a prayer for her safety. After he respectfully closed his prayer, a cloud floated over the moon removing the beam of light from her window. With a broad grin on his face, General Von joyously thought: *This is a good omen! The light of the moon was quickly retrieved and transmitted back to heaven along with my prayer.* It was also a calming thought for him that perhaps Rachel was thinking of home at the very same time the beam of light from heaven was upon her window.

*****

Early the next morning, General Von and Adam left the island of Lantau and traveled by Chinese junk up the Pearl River to Canton. He had hoped for a faster sailing vessel to traverse the short distance as time was the most important factor in this whole operation. He knew General Tso was expecting the shipment of opium in the course of a few weeks. General Von stood on the boat deck critically gazing up and down at the length of the boat as it lumbered against the current of the river. It was very unwieldy and deadweight in the water. The general thought, *yes, the junk served its purpose many years ago as the formidable warship of the Chinese and proved its worth in the Far East, along side the Viking long boats and the Roman galleys, but speed is of the essence, now.* He tried to contain his nervous reaction to the slow moving boat. He gave himself a stern pep talk to remain calm and to keep his mind free from stress… *if possible.*

CHAPTER ELEVEN

It was mid-afternoon when the junk moored into a slip in Canton. Adam slept most of the journey curled up on a large coil of heavy rope, while General Von paced the deck for hours, swishing his riding crop back and forth, as if in his own little trance, talking to no one, and seeing nothing. He was abruptly startled by seamen hurriedly moving on deck, making ready to secure the boat by rope to the wharf, and he quickly moved to the starboard side of the vessel for safety. Adam was hustled off his makeshift bed of rope and stood quietly beside the general. Both looked down at the swirling, muddy water of the Pearl River then gazed across the length of the wharf at the other ships that were moored.

Merciful heaven, I don't believe it! General Von joyously thought. *It can't be. It is! It's the Ladybug! I never thought a tramp steamer could look so beautiful.* General Von tried to hide his excitement from Adam as the two stood side-by-side ready to disembark the junk. He was eager to find out if Captain Leif Oscarson was still master of the *Ladybug* and, if so, he intended to board the ship after dark when Adam was asleep.

The general and Adam walked the streets of Canton going in and out of several buildings in an effort to find a reputable hotel in close proximity to the wharf area. This was no easy task. Finally, the general settled on one dilapidated hotel that was located a few blocks away from the river and within a short walking distance from where the *Ladybug* was docked. He booked two rooms on the second floor where there was no view of the river from either room. General Von did not want Adam to have the opportunity to see the *Ladybug* from his window where he could spy on his midnight rendezvous with Captain Oscarson.

*****

Captain Oscarson and General Von were old friends who were caught in a web of intrigue and gold smuggling in Macau, which culminated in an attempt by General Tso and the Chinese Triad to kidnap Rachel while she was aboard the *Ladybug*. Both carry responsibility and authority with the grace of a bird floating on the morning breeze. Both exemplify a bellicose personality when commanding men, and at the same time receive the greatest respect from their men. Their moral values are identical, striving to defend their reputation with courage and honor.

The *S/S Ladybug* was an old tramp steamer, or merchant vessel, that had been powered by steam and recently converted to diesel engine. It was of Swedish registry and it sailed wherever there was cargo to be shipped, operating without a schedule. Each voyage was separately negotiated between the ship's owner and the shipper. The articles of agreement between the master of the ship and its seamen specified the vessel could sail to ports and places in any part of the world as the master may direct and must return to the port of discharge in a term of time not exceeding twelve months. It was prohibited for seamen to go on shore in foreign ports except by permission of the master. Rules were stringent and strictly enforced.

*****

Light from flickering lamps along the wharf cast weird shadows on the dock with only an occasional lap of water against the wharf breaking the silence. The Pearl River looked even more ominous at night, as if it were a living monster… almost vicious as the muddy water vigorously swirled, daring anyone or anything to invade its dominion at its own peril. There was no activity on any of the ships moored... and all was quiet.

General Von waited long into the night, making certain Adam was asleep, before he quietly left his room and walked the short distance to the *Ladybug.*

"Who goes there?" a sailor on watch called in a strong, deep voice.

General Von quickly walked up the ship's plank and said in a whisper, "If Captain Oscarson is master of this ship, I would like to see him."

"At this hour?" the sailor retorted.

"Yes. Tell him a very old friend from the island of Lantau would like to see him."

General Von stood quietly on deck while the sailor reluctantly left his post to deliver the message. A few minutes later, two men approached... the sailor and Captain Oscarson.

"Well, old friend, I didn't expect to see you so soon." Captain Oscarson, had a broad grin on his face, extended his hand to offer a warm handshake and questioned, "and why a visit late at night?" He chuckled to add, "I am a more gracious host during the day."

The sailor took his post on deck, and General Von quickly escorted the captain to the far side of the ship to be out of sight from anyone on the dock.

The broad grin on the captain's face sharply changed to a solemn stare when he noticed through the dim lamp light the heavy worried lines on the general's face. His instincts told him this was not a happy visit. He was anxious to hear what was troubling the general and he wondered why the urgency for a late-night visit. The captain could feel the general's pain and he grievously said, "I think you have much to tell me."

CHAPTER TWELVE

With belabored speech, the general slowly divulged the confidential plot General Tso had planned for the shipment of opium from Canton to Panama, which included holding his daughter hostage in Japan until safe transfer of the shipment. General Von quickly explained that Sydney and Quan Lee were already in the Tokyo/Yokohama area, acting upon their instructions to contact Chang in Chinatown. When the general mentioned that Seth was expected to arrive in Japan the next day from Korea to assist with Rachel's capture, Captain Oscarson questioned the general at great length, expressing enthusiasm to see his young friend again.

Many minutes later and with regret, the general informed the captain that one of his lieutenants was with him in Canton… only as a way of keeping a close watch on him as he had sold vital information to the Triad leading to Rachel's kidnapping. At this point in relating his plans, the general paused, swished his riding crop vigorously in the air, and vehemently said, "That son of a bitch! His face repulses me. I don't like being alone with him in the same room. I'm afraid I'll strangle him with my bare hands."

Captain Oscarson stood quietly at the railing of the ship with the soft, cool, river breeze fanning his face. He did not want to break the general's tirade of speech. He knew the general was speaking friend-to-friend, baring his soul as friends are want to do.

The general took a deep breath, sighed, and slowly began, "Life is ironic, isn't it?" Not wanting an answer he continued, "You have a young man... Adam, one of my most capable lieutenants who had a brilliant future ahead of him working for the British Intelligence office and he squandered it... all for love."

Captain Oscarson turned to look directly at the general with a questioning gaze.

"Oh, yes," the general said with a sobering realization, "Adam professed his love to Rachel and she turned him down. Love and hate are strange bedfellows... where one can quickly turn on the other. Adam chose to sell his soul to the devil in order to hurt Rachel as he had been hurt. He is pregnant with evil and I know it will continue to grow as he has tasted the luxury of having money in his pocket. I fear he will always conceive trouble."

"My friend, we must use caution," the captain admonished. "We don't want to tip our hand that we know the Triad has an informant in our camp. Let me tell you what I know about this particular shipment of opium to Panama."

General Von's expression changed quickly to a look of surprise. He quieted his inner turmoil of frustration and listened eagerly and intently to the captain expound with alacrity.

"When I arrived in Canton a few days ago and unloaded the ship's cargo, I was contacted by a Japanese young man who represented Sun Enterprises in Tokyo. The young man had checked with the shipping commissioner in Canton and was told I was sailing to Yokohama with sufficient cargo, and possibly the *Ladybug* could carry an additional small shipment. He explained the main source of revenue for Sun Enterprises was shipping agricultural products, and he wanted to know if the *Ladybug* could handle a relatively small shipment of barrels of rice. I, of course, was happy to have my ship carry a full cargo in the hold and told him I would accept the barrels of rice for shipment to Yokohama.

"Since I had never transported cargo for Sun Enterprises, I conducted a little research regarding the financial status of this company, which is customary in the shipping business."

Captain Oscarson stopped at this point to ask the general if he would like a cup of coffee or perhaps a shot of vodka to keep them both alert. The general declined the offer as he was eager to hear the rest of the story.

"Sun Enterprises is principally owned and operated by Sun Lo. After a little research, I found out that Sun Lo is one of the most nefarious criminals in all of Japan, who deals in every vice known to mankind."

Captain Oscarson looked squarely at the general and with a strong caveat continued, "It hasn't been too long ago that the *Ladybug* was used to transfer Hitler's gold from France to Macau… unbeknownst to me!" And emphatically added, "Never again do I want to become involved with any illegal cargo being shipped!"

The captain turned and left the deck for a few minutes, leaving the general anxious to hear more. When the captain returned, he held two small shot glasses of vodka in his hands and offered one to the general.

"It was just this afternoon that I accepted the small cargo of barrels of rice. I had it stored close to the hatch of the hold so I could secretly open one of the barrels to see for myself if anything was being smuggled inside. Lo and behold, bags of opium were hidden deep inside the barrels. None of the crew knows of this and I intend to keep it that way. There is no need to involve anyone else as I intend to turn the cargo over to the authorities in Yokohama as soon as we drop anchor."

With a big grin on his face, Captain Oscarson joyfully exclaimed, "General, I think you arrived at the most opportune time… how fortuitous!"

General Von couldn't believe his ears. He was exhilarated with his good fortune. He thought… *time is of the essence and we are on a good schedule.*

Both men raised their vodka glasses and made a toast for their good luck to continue, for both men knew that General Tso would never surrender Rachel.

CHAPTER THIRTEEN

It was almost daybreak when General Von returned to the hotel. He quietly stopped at the door to Adam's room to listen for any movement. He heard nothing and walked to his room at the far end of the dark hallway. He wanted to sleep for awhile before breakfast with Adam, but his mind raced with excitement for the plan to evolve, which he and Captain Oscarson had devised. It was a plan, which miraculously developed on its own with all facets neatly falling into place at the same time. He went over the circumstances in his head... *Of all the ships in Canton, it was the Ladybug, helmed by my good friend Captain Oscarson, which would carry the opium; and by coincidence, Adam and I arrived in Canton at the perfect time to sail on the ship as if to provide a safe delivery of opium to Yokohama.* He cynically smiled and thought... *as if I am conceding to General Tso's demand for safe passage of his cargo.* Then, as if talking to General Tso, he continued... *I promise... you will feel my wrath before this is over.*

An hour later, General Von decided to fetch Adam for breakfast. He hadn't fallen to sleep anyway and he was anxious for the day to begin. During breakfast, the general casually informed Adam: "I had a late-night visitor."

Adam showed no facial emotions upon hearing the news, made no comment, and continued eating his breakfast with his head bowed over his plate.

"I was shocked at first to learn the messenger was a member of the Chinese Triad, which indicated to me they knew I had arrived in Canton, and they knew where I had booked lodging."

Adam continued eating, making no sign of concern.

"I was told the opium was being shipped to Yokohama today on the *Ladybug,* and arrangements have been made for both of us to sail this afternoon."

There was no sign of reaction from Adam.

General Von was livid with hatred for Adam's lack of response to hearing this news, which clearly enforced the general's opinion that Adam knew he would be contacted somewhere in Canton with instructions from General Tso. There was no doubt Adam had informed the Triad of General Von's course of action for both of them to travel to Canton, which prepared the hoodlums to await their arrival.

To continue the charade, General Von brightly continued, "This is great news! Now, I can personally see to it that the opium will arrive safely in Yokohama." He drew a deep breath, sighed and said, "...and then Rachel will be released."

There were a few minutes when nothing was said. The general imagined Adam was quietly basking in his cleverness as a traitor.

A slight smile parted the general's lips when he thought: *Adam, you are sitting in that chair thinking how very smart you are in contributing to this vile hostage caper. The reality is I know about your plans... and you bloody bastard... you are being duped.*

"Adam, I believe the Triad is like an octopus with its many tentacles of hoodlums stretched in all directions monitoring my every move. I'll have to give them credit... they are clever."

The two men finished breakfast with no further conversation. As anticipated, Adam asked to be excused from the breakfast table to purchase a pack of cigarettes.

The general knew Adam was going to contact a member of the Triad with the good news that the opium shipment would arrive safely in Yokohama.

CHAPTER FOURTEEN

A rather large rectangular-shaped window furnishes light for the dismal cell, but it is a little too high in the wall to provide a view. Rachel quickly discovered by moving the iron cot under the window, she could balance on the head railing and see outside. She recognized nothing. The window affords a view of a harbor, which is several hundred yards away and a long row of four-story warehouses along the wharf. She surmises she is on the first floor of a similar building.

The cold, damp air in the cell penetrates her body and she shivers. She is wearing the typical Chinese loose-fitting black woolen trousers with the customary piece of garment hanging in front down to the ankles, like an apron, and another piece hanging behind in the same way. Her long black jacket with wide sleeves reaches her knees and all garments provide warmth, but it is her frazzled nerves that contribute to the shivers and the fear of her predicament.

Rachel flops down on the cot and is surprised to feel something poking her in the side. She reaches under her jacket and pulls a sheathed knife, which she always secured to the belt of her trousers when she was on a surveillance assignment for her father. She thinks: *How can this be? Did my captors fail to frisk me?* and in deeper contemplation: *This is their first mistake!* A renewed feeling of strength surges through her body at the thought of having a knife that she can use against her assailants when necessary.

Jeannine Dahlberg

Her short-term memory is slowly returning, but she has no depth perception… there are only seconds when flashes of memory return jolting her conscious awareness. The fiercely throbbing headache caused by the blow to her head has finally gone; and after an opportunity to wash the bloody tangle from her hair, she is beginning to feel better.

She receives a pan of food twice daily, which is brought to her by a Japanese guard, who always mumbled something as he placed the pan on the floor, but she neither looks at him nor gives a response. A lighted candle is brought to her every evening, which she promptly places on the windowsill, hoping to attract someone… anyone… who can help her. She has not seen the two Chinese men who kidnapped her from the parade in Hong Kong and brought her to Japan since the first day she opened her eyes in the cell-like room in the warehouse. Her thoughts turn to the one Chinese man who came to her rescue when the other sought to ravish her. *If I could only see him again, perhaps I know him.* With these thoughts going through her mind, the stone floor beneath her feet shakes, the room vibrates and the iron cot rattles. She cries: *Oh, God! What's happening, now?* Tears roll down her cheeks.

*****

Both men spoke in Mandarin Chinese and it was quite evident they were irritated. "I don't like this one bit. We've already been in Japan too long. If Yokohama did not have a large Chinatown district, I'd be out of here. I don't like mingling with the Japanese. I know my ancestors would not approve." Wang bellowed.

"Keep your voice down," Chang pleaded. "I don't want the guard to hear you. We have enough to worry about without begging more problems."

Their mission was simple. Sun Lo, leader of one of the largest gangs of drug traffickers in the Tokyo/Yokohama area, asked that they check on Rachel to make certain she has not been harmed in any way and to report to him immediately. Chang was fortunate to overhear a conversation between Sun Lo and General Tso that Rachel was to be transferred to a ship bound for Panama very shortly. Chang was surprised to learn that General Tso had come to Yokohama from Panama to handle Rachel's transfer. Indeed, Rachel's abduction was a coup for General Tso and he wanted to handle the details himself.

As the two men were about to enter Rachel's cell, Chang yelled in Pidgin English in a frightened, high-pitched voice, "Holy molely! Floor move! You right, Wang. Japan no good very bad awful place for us."

While opening the steel door to Rachel's cell, the Japanese guard laughed, mocking the two Chinese men and spoke in Japanese, which neither one understands. "Are you afraid of a little earth tremor? This is nothing. How brave will you be when a full-scale earthquake shakes the ground and moves the waves?" The Japanese guard continued laughing at Wang and Chang while returning to his desk at the end of the hall.

Again, Chang spoke, "They crazy people here. They laugh at tsunami… big wave come fast. We no want be here!"

Rachel cannot believe her ears. She knows that voice and the Pidgin English. It's Chang!

The two men enter the room… neither one wanting to linger long. The floor stops moving, but all three hesitate to speak as fear of a full-fledged earthquake consumes their thoughts. The people of China are well aware of the many earthquakes and seismic waves that plague Japan, and they stand quietly for a few seconds hoping another tremor will not come. Fear and apprehension freeze the three. No one moves.

Wang had hoped to finish what he had started with Rachel; but on second thought, he looked around the cell, took a long, lustful look at Rachel and left the room.

A faint smile betrays the tenderness Chang feels for Rachel and he speaks in Pidgin English, "Sun Lo hope you well. You leave soon." And with a wink of his eye he continues, "Not to worry."

Wang was standing outside the cell door and asked Chang, "What was that all about? What gibberish were you speaking?"

Chang answers, "Oh, I know fine English. Learn from American fly boys during big war."

The two men hurriedly leave the warehouse, wanting to distance themselves from the harbor area just in case there is a tidal wave from the small earth tremor.

The thrill of seeing Chang is almost more than Rachel can bear. She wants to cheer with happiness. She vows there will be no more tears. The dark phantom of her imagination will no longer haunt her as her spirits sore to new heights. There is hope.

CHAPTER FIFTEEN

Major Tamermia was surprised to see a beehive of activity when he entered the command tent late morning. The battalion commanding officer was studying the many area maps on the table locating the enemy according to recent reconnaissance information, while the staff sergeant directed men to pack the equipment. They were on the move again. He talked briefly and quietly with the commanding officer and then walked to the rear of the tent where Seth was finishing typing the last of the special courts-martial cases.

With a big, broad grin on his face, the major slowly and deliberately said, "Corporal, you have friends in high places! You have received orders from the Pentagon and co-signed by General Dean that you are to move out immediately."

The major continued staring at Seth and did not say another word for a few seconds. Seth became very uneasy under the major's scrutiny and with a baffled, quizzical look questioned the major, "What do you mean, sir?"

"You have been ordered to take your R-and-R immediately. Pack your gear, corporal. You're leaving from Kimpo Airbase outside Seoul, South Korea, where you will catch a plane for Japan. You may be gone longer than the regular five-day leave time for R-and-R so prepare for a longer stay." The major paused for a moment thinking, *I wonder if I will ever see the corporal again,* and continued, "It looks like you will be heading south to Seoul while we will be going north… to the Iron Triangle area."

Seth was confused by the request. First, the orders came from the Pentagon; and second, what was the urgent need for him to go to Japan immediately; and third, who requested his leave.

"Corporal, I have been advised you will be contacted when you arrive in Yokohama, Japan, and will receive further orders at that time. The name General Erik von Horstmann was mentioned… and that's all I know."

The major turned to his desk to begin the process of packing all papers, preparing for the impending move, while Seth closed his typewriter and handed it to the soldier in charge of loading the truck. Everyone worked quickly and by chow time the tent was empty, leaving Seth and the major alone to finish packing the briefs.

Jumbled thoughts raced through Seth's mind upon hearing General Erik von Horstmann's name. *Has his premonition materialized? Has something happened to Rachel?*

"Corporal, I have no idea what this is all about and you certainly don't have to tell me anything, but I've told you that you remind me of my kid brother and I guess I want to take responsibility for your safety. Have you ever heard of General Erik von Horstmann?"

"Yes, sir, I have. General Von is my girlfriend's father. The general commands the post, which also doubles as an orphanage, on the island of Lantau leading the fight against gold smugglers and drug traffickers in the Hong Kong, Macau and Canton areas at the request of both the British Intelligence and the French Interpol offices. You see, sir, this is why I have been worried about Rachel. She serves as one of the orphanage administrators, devoting her time and energy in a loving way to create an atmosphere of happiness and hope for the many orphaned children. But she also likes to become involved with the dangerous aspects of helping to clean up the evil element of people who threaten the young people of China; and on occasion, she runs errands and does surveillance for the general when the operation is deemed safe. I knew something was wrong when I hadn't heard from her after a few weeks."

The major questioned, "How did it happen that you met Rachel… and in China of all places?"

Quick, loving, tender thoughts of Rachel flashed through his mind and he answered, "You never know where you are going to meet the love of your life;" and questioned, "do you believe in love at first sight?"

"I guess I never took the time to develop any kind of a relationship with a girl, as my first love has always been to fulfill my military obligation and to serve my country as a soldier, which is a natural feeling... almost instinctive... coming from a long line of military ancestors."

The major sat down in the one remaining chair in the tent; took out a cigarette and after blowing a few smoke rings, continued. "I grew up in a military household... I guess you could call me an army brat... but the military lineage emanates with my great grandfather. The conversation at the table after dinner was always filled with exciting stories of battles, heroism, honor, loyalty; and to a youngster, I knew no other way of life. The men in our family were to follow the code of the military... and I would have it no other way.

"My great grandfather was fourteen when he fought with the Union Army at Gettysburg in 1863. That was the largest Civil War battle ever waged and he survived the bloody bayonet charge led by General Reynolds of the famous Iron Brigade. After the Civil War, he joined the cavalry under Lieutenant Colonel George Armstrong Custer and fought in the battle of the Little Big Horn." The major took a few more puffs from his cigarette; blew a few more smoke rings and said, "And, of course, you know that was Custer's Last Stand where all the soldiers were killed. Can you imagine a battalion of one hundred ninety-seven men facing the largest concentration of Indians... twenty-five hundred warriors...? The Indians' encampment on the Little Big Horn River was the largest ever recorded representing six tribes with an estimated ten to fifteen thousand Indians." The major's sentence trailed off as he envisioned the horrendous battle scene.

Seth sat quietly on a box of courts-martial cases captivated by the major's description of the battle. He could easily recognize the stories had an emotional impact on the major and he did not want to break his reverie. The major had never carried on a long conversation with him on any subject; and Seth held the major in such high esteem that he felt honored to be made aware of his family's history.

"My grandfather was in the Spanish American War of 1898 and served in the navy aboard the battleship *Maine*. It was only a second-class battleship, but it was the largest ship ever to enter Havana harbor, and the Cubans thought it was a floating American fortress. The ship was mysteriously blown up and my grandfather was one of the seamen who was killed. Oh, there was an investigation, but nothing was ever discovered nor was anyone ever held responsible. All we had after that was the slogan, 'Remember the *Maine*.'

"And my father was in the war to end all wars... World War I. He was in the bloody trench warfare at the battle of Verdun. He, too, was killed.

"Corporal, I guess somewhere along the line the glory has gone out of wars... at least for me. The stories I heard as a young boy were all told gloriously, where we knew what we were fighting for and we wanted to serve our country. Of course, I don't have to tell you about World War II. I'm sure you remember all the battles... and I fought in many of the bloody engagements... D-day, the battle of the Bulge... well, suffice it to say, I saw my share of action.

"But, corporal, you know, this war in Korea has me baffled. They don't call it a war, but men are dying. It's called a police action and the battles we fight on the many hills have no names. The hills are numbered... with the exception of a few... such as Pork Chop Hill and Old Baldy. I haven't mentioned to you that my kid brother was killed here a few months ago."

With that thought, the major stopped. His voice trembled and he could not continue. He took his handkerchief from his pocket, wiped his eyes, blew his nose and in a mournful tone said, "All the Tamermia men were killed in wars, but somehow they all found time to marry and have children. I think it's my time to retire from the military and settle down. Now that my kid brother was killed, I guess it's up to me to have some little Tamermias to carry on our good name." More tears welled in his eyes. "Corporal, I don't know what got me started on my family history. I think I asked you how you met Rachel."

"Like you, sir, I was raised in a family that placed honor and loyalty above everything else. My grandfather told me over and over again that you're only as good as your word; and if you can't stand behind your word, you're a nobody. Major, your loyalty was to the military. Three generations of Colemans devoted their energy, loyalty and respect to the Ramsey family who were owners of a very large tobacco plantation in Virginia. I say were owners because after the matriarch of the family, Miss Patti, died, it was believed there were no more Ramseys to inherit the plantation and the vast holdings in the commodities market. At this time, my dad was the director and principal manager of the plantation and he believed there was a daughter born in Paris to the Ramsey son shortly before World War II. The baby daughter was placed in an orphanage in Paris after both parents died… the mother died at childbirth and the father was killed.

"Shortly after the War, and after I graduated college, my dad asked me to go to Paris to see if I could find any records substantiating the birth of a baby girl. He wanted to explore every possible lead and to fulfill his obligation to the Ramsey family. Dad figured the girl would be about nineteen years old, so you can understand all records of her birth would be very old and difficult to trace." Seth paused in his story, shook his head in disbelief, and in an amazed tone of voice said, "That journey led me to an investigation that was the once-in-a-lifetime adventure.

"From Paris, I traveled aboard the *Ladybug*, which is a tramp steamer, to Hong Kong. To paraphrase the adventure in the vernacular of the Chinese: *I was riding the tail of the dragon.* I was whipped all around the world… and good luck traveled with me all the way."

Seth started pacing around the tent as if reliving every profound, exciting experience of the investigation. His narration was thorough in every detail and his speech was filled with enthusiasm.

"The first time I saw Rachel, she was maneuvering a sampan along side the *Ladybug* while the ship was at anchor in Victoria Harbor in Hong Kong."

Seth stopped to remember how beautiful Rachel looked in the early morning as the rays of the sun bounced across the water onto her sampan. The vision still takes his breath away.

"Major, it was love at first sight!"

"Corporal, that's quite a story. I'd like to meet Rachel someday."

The commotion of the soldiers leaving the mess tent interrupted their conversation.

"Corporal, we had better brake for lunch now if we expect to get anything to eat. We're finished here and we have all the court briefs packed. We will be ready to move north." With a strong caveat, the major cautioned Seth: "I want you to be careful in Japan. You're a good soldier and I want you to report to me as soon as you return."

The two soldiers said their last good-byes.

CHAPTER SIXTEEN

"Hey, man! Where have you been?" Ian called as Seth entered his tent. "Our unit is moving out, and guess what? I've served the time and I have enough duty points to get out of here for a few days... I'm goin' to Japan! Those poor guys are goin' north and I'm headin' for some fun and relaxation." Ian danced around, clapping his hands in a rhythmic beat, poked Seth on the arm and jokingly said, "Now, don't get jealous."

"Oh, I'm not jealous... I'm going with you."

Ian stopped his dance and questioned, "What? I thought you figured the other night that you don't have enough points for R-and-R."

"Well, Ian, the army knows that someone should look after you and keep you an honorable man." Seth had a big grin on his face and poked Ian on the arm.

Both men stood looking and smiling at one another relishing the thought that they would be leaving the war for awhile.

Ian became thoughtful and acknowledged, "You must have friends in high places... or perhaps your lucky dragon is still riding with you." Ian laughed.

Seth flashed Ian a quizzical stare, thinking... *Let's hope so.*

*****

The ride in an open truck with only a canvas cover to protect the soldiers from the cold wind was another exhilarating experience. The truck was crowded with soldiers who were leaving their units for a few days to begin their rest-and-recuperation time in Japan. They had earned their points in combat and were now eligible for a few days leave when they could be free from worry and stress of the war. The mood of the men was festive and boisterous. They wanted to enjoy every second... beginning now.

Seth reflected upon the first day he arrived in Pusan, South Korea. The soldiers were quickly hustled aboard a train, which was driven by a steam engine. They sat on wooden benches in crowded railroad cars as the train laboriously chugged north to the fighting area. The temperament of the men was quite different at that time. The soldiers were extremely quiet and deep in their own thoughts, which were filled with anxiety, and their nerves were strained with the dread of not knowing how far north and how close to the enemy line they were being taken. The surrounding landscape gave the soldiers their first visual contact of the devastation and destruction war can graphically paint... a picture these men had never seen. With the sound of every clickedy-clack of the train wheels on the tracks, they knew their life never would be the same. They could hear the big guns... and then the machine guns... and they knew war was just a little farther up the tracks.

Seth quickly jolted his depressive thoughts to the present, where happier men were starting to unwind, trying to forget everything about the war, and wanting to enjoy every moment away from the fighting. He had no knowledge of why he had been called to Japan, but he assumed it had something to do with Rachel. Seth was determined to put a positive spin on his thoughts and believe that Rachel was safe. He thought to himself: *If believing will make it so... then so be it.*

The truck ride was not comfortable as it bounced along the road, but the jovial environment created by the soldiers helped to make the drive along the Han River to Seoul, South Korea, seem short when they arrived at Kimpo Air Base in Seoul. The soldiers were happy to see a huge airplane already on the tarmac waiting to take the men to Japan. There would be no delay.

Ian wrinkled his brow and pondered, "Have you ever seen a bigger airplane? I've heard about these flying boxcars, but I've never seen one. I sure hope it will hang in the sky until we reach Japan."

The aircraft was loaded quickly as soldiers hustled to board the converted cargo plane… eager to sit in bucket seats, which were lined against the sides of the fuselage. Under every third seat was a deflated rubber life raft, which was to be inflated if the plane were shot down over the Sea of Japan. Each soldier was given a parachute to wear with quick instructions of how to use the parachute if the plane sustained enemy fire. The soldiers were still in a festive mood and good-naturedly bantered around the purpose of the parachute as no one had ever jumped from a plane. They all jokingly decided each man would push the man in front of him out the plane. To the roar of jubilant voices, the plane landed safely at the Yokota Air Force Base, located near Camp Zama, which is in the Tankard Mountain Range in Japan.

Ian sat near the door of the plane and was one of the first to leave. He gave a quick glance to Seth, who was farther back in the tail of the plane, and called, "Man, that was some ride! I'm outa here."

Seth grabbed his duffel bag and stood in line awaiting his turn to leave the plane. He noticed a sergeant standing on the tarmac next to the ramp as the soldiers departed… questioning each one. As he approached the foot of the ramp, he could hear the sergeant asking their name and passing each man along his way.

Seth stepped off the ramp and reported, "Corporal Seth Coleman, sir." and continued walking.

The sergeant called, "Halt right there, corporal. The colonel wants to see you."

CHAPTER SEVENTEEN

Seth followed the sergeant's orders to follow the road to the first building at the left of the concrete barracks. He marveled at all the concrete construction that was in process as he walked quickly to the colonel's office. His college degree in architecture fortified his love of architectural design, which enabled him to be ever conscious of new construction. He walked slowly admiring a unique two-story building, which was nearing completion. It appeared to be designed after the Pentagon building in Washington, D. C. Later, he learned that the camp was to become a processing center for all military personnel, whether coming in or leaving the Tokyo area.

His thoughts were reminiscent of an on-going daydream when he becomes a world-renowned architect and leaves a legacy of beautiful buildings. It was these thoughts that often sustained him during times of depression… the murderous brutality of war… and being separated from Rachel. He was deep in his thoughts of Rachel when he entered the colonel's office.

Seth saluted the colonel and called out, "Corporal Coleman reporting, sir." He stood at attention for a full minute, which felt to Seth more like ten minutes, before the colonel spoke. Seth gazed straight ahead while the colonel piercingly scrutinized the young soldier before him. The colonel pranced around his desk with a hubristic demeanor, thinking sarcastically: *Who does this young, raw soldier know in the Pentagon?*

In a forceful voice, resonating authority, the smug colonel bellowed, "Corporal, I have received orders from the Pentagon that you are to be taken immediately to the Chinatown district in Yokohama. I have a jeep ready to drive you to the area. There are four colorful gates that stand at the entrances and I have been instructed to drive you to the northern most gate where someone will meet you. I assume this person knows you." The colonel's tone of voice indicated that he was unhappy with not being privy to more details. He was accustomed to having complete control over all operations involving the men under his command... except when the Pentagon issued orders. And with a feeling of contempt, he continued, "Now, you know as much as I do."

The colonel called to the outer office commanding the private to place a phone call to a number given to him by the Pentagon. When the line was connected, the colonel delivered the message as instructed, which was quick and to the point. "He's on his way."

Seth was happy to leave the colonel's office. He felt very uncomfortable in his presence and quickly surmised the colonel's character was one of grasping power and flaunting arrogance... a combination that was definitely difficult for men serving under him to respect. It made Seth realize how lucky he was to have Major Tamermia as his superior officer.

While Seth waited outside for his ride to Yokohama, his thoughts ran rampant in flashes depicting scenes of what may lie ahead, which were all distressing thoughts as he did not know what to expect. He wondered if he would have the good fortune he experienced in locating Rachel in China... where he encountered one dangerous predicament after another... and good luck was always with him.

Seth recalled his unnerving voyage from Le Havre, France, to Hong Kong, China, aboard a tramp steamer, the *Ladybug,* where his knowledge of the mystical beliefs of the Far East was greatly expanded. Tender thoughts linger in his memory as he contemplates the many long conversations he had with the captain of the ship, Captain Oscarson, who became his mentor. The captain's voluminous knowledge opened a broad dimension of many new subjects holding Seth captivated with his stories of ancient Chinese culture. His dad had warned him he would experience culture shock when he arrived in China, and it was the captain who explained how Old World modes of thought are bogged down in centuries of traditional celebrations where rituals and ceremonies are rooted in the past. Seth became fascinated with the mythical lore of the dragon, which continues to perpetuate a rigid discipline practiced by many Chinese people today. The dragon is placed among the deified forces of nature, having powers of the air; symbolizing power, fertility, health, prosperity… creating a beneficent creature. The dragon was the emblem of the Imperial family, adorning the Chinese flag until 1911. Seth's many long conversations with the captain aboard ship, forged a similar belief, as the captain had said: *the universe is a university where our choices in life determine our consequences.* He allowed his imagination of the mythical lore of the Chinese dragon to protect him and to be his benefactor… and he found Rachel. His childhood religious training enforced his belief that there are no coincidences… it is God's way of allowing something good to happen. He was not afraid to die… no more than he was to be born. He believed that with both the omnipotent power of God and the mythical power of the dragon, his good fortune would continue. He knew he would need all the help he could get.

CHAPTER EIGHTEEN

Private Mitchell drove the jeep to a screeching stop in front of the colonel's office. Seth threw his duffel bag on the back seat and hopped up front listening to the motor rev and the two sped off for Yokohama. *I've survived the war zone. Now, I hope I survive this ride to Chinatown.* Considering it was a rather wild ride, the private was quite talkative, explaining he was a recent college graduate majoring in history of the Far East with his goal of becoming a professor at Stanford University. With both hands grasped tightly to the jeep, while the private negotiated some fancy maneuvering over the bumpy road, Seth listened as the private gave him a guided tour of the landscape. Seth smiled, appreciating a one-sided conversation that had nothing to do with the war or his impending meeting in Chinatown. There was no way he could relax in the jeep, but he found the ride to be quite invigorating… if not fun.

The private was quite knowledgeable of the history of Yokohama and explained: "In May 1945, the Pacific Front of World War II moved to Japanese soil. Yokohama, which was one of the most famous port cities in the world at that time, was destroyed by Allied air strikes and lost more than half of the port facilities.

"It was not always a thriving port. In earlier centuries, it was an obscure fishing village on the southwestern coast of Tokyo Bay, where the ruler, known as the Shogunate, strictly enforced an isolation policy when no one was allowed out of the country or into the country except for a few Dutch traders. In the nineteenth century, Commodore Matthew Perry arrived in the harbor with two steam-driven warships. The Japanese, realizing they were technologically inferior to the Americans, allowed the ships to enter the bay as they would be hard pressed to defend themselves against such powerful cannons and warships. A year later, Perry returned and the Japanese signed the Kanagawa Treaty opening two ports to the American ships; and a few years later, the US-Japan Treaty of Amity was signed opening more ports to foreign trade.

"It was at this time that the Chinatown district in central Yokohama developed and expanded to become the largest Chinese settlement in Japan. It became a thriving community for stores and restaurants."

Seth assumed the private was honing his teaching skills, as the conversation had now turned into a lecture. He continued to be attentive while enjoying the plethora of ancient temples and historical sites scattered over the landscape. Seth wanted to ask the private about one temple in particular, but thought it best not to interrupt his monologue. He knew he was a captive audience.

It was evident the private appreciated someone to talk to… someone who would listen while he expanded on Japanese history. The private was enjoying the drive into Yokohama and he continued.

"World War II came to an end for Japan in August 1945. Shortly after surrender, over five hundred military officers committed suicide and many hundreds more were executed for committing war crimes. Occupation by the Allied Powers started with General Douglas MacArthur… its first supreme commander. The concept of a 'New Japan' was quickly promulgated; and for many Japanese it was a welcomed change from living under a totalitarian regime. For others, this was the first time their land had been occupied by foreign powers and they thought everything had been lost. To their surprise, the nation quickly demonstrated its ability to recover physically, economically and culturally from the apparent disaster. The emperor lost all political and military power and a constitution went into effect."

The lecture abruptly stopped as the private slowed in speed when they entered the narrow streets of the city. Pedestrians crowded close to the jeep with lively interest and curious stares as the two American soldiers slowly proceeded with great caution to the Chinatown district in central Yokohama. They could see the tops of the colorful gates, but it was a circuitous route on winding roads that led to the four entrances, which mark the boundaries of Chinatown proper. Seth was happy not to be driving while the private nervously negotiated steering the jeep through the melee of pedestrians while searching for the northern most gate. Seth's interest was drawn to the buildings lining the streets in the area, which had suffered great devastation from the war, and were still in the process of being restored. Construction workers were busily moving piles of debris with heavy equipment, pickaxes and shovels. Men were hustling all over the area reminding Seth of bees in a beehive. Much work was still to be done to restore it to the viable port city it was before the war, and it was evident they were anxious to get the job done.

The private made a sharp turn onto a street that appeared to be going nowhere... suddenly, looming one block away before them, was the north gate.

"This is it," called the private flashing a friendly smile and offering a handshake. "I sure enjoyed our conversation, which made it a fast trip."

Seth extended his hand, quickly responding, "Yeah, thanks for the ride." Seth thought: *You talked; I listened. Conversation?*

Seth grabbed his duffel bag from the back seat and proceeded to walk slowly, not knowing who or what to expect. Fortunately, there were not many people meandering in the immediate vicinity of the north entrance. His extra precautionary senses were fortified by the adrenalin pumping through his veins as the vivid, wild crimson stories he had heard from soldiers who had returned from R and R were now plaguing him with irritating thoughts. He quickly glanced in all directions with sharp eyes...hoping to see someone he would possibly recognize. He gasped with pleasure and disbelief when he saw a familiar figure standing beside the colorful column at the wide entrance.

I don't believe it!

CHAPTER NINETEEN

"Chang! What are you doing here in Japan?" Seth called in a loud voice unable to contain his excitement. He never expected to see this coolie again after he left Hong Kong. With a wide grin on his face and a long stride, he walked quickly to the entrance, holding out his arms as if to embrace him.

Chang stood quietly beside his rickshaw, showing absolutely no emotion, and quickly stepped backward with a grimace and a frightened look on his face. Seth quizzically thought: *How can this be? Certainly, he hasn't forgotten the many wild, narrow escapes we experienced together in Hong Kong. He saved my life more than once. When I left Hong Kong, there was a strong feeling between us of a tight brotherly bond. What happened?*

Chang motioned for Seth to get into the rickshaw, which was a small covered vehicle supported by long bamboo poles and two wheels attached to a bicycle, and quietly cautioned, "I no want to get us killed." And with a gleam in his eye, continued, "Not to worry. You still number one best friend. We talk later."

Chang zigzagged his way through the crowded pedestrian-filled narrow streets, reminding Seth of watching salmon swim upstream against the forceful current of the river. Hanging red lanterns swayed in the breeze across the streets; garish, colorful designs decorated the storefronts of tradesmen offering their services of tailoring, barbering and cooking; curio shops, herbalists, import boutiques;

replete with restaurants and tea salons completed the scenario of a bustling hub of commercial activity.

Chang was a street-wise kid who peddled the streets as if he owned them. For Seth, this ride through Chinatown was reminiscent of his rickshaw rides in Hong Kong, where Chang was equally adept at running through the streets unscathed. Chang appeared to know many of the shop owners, as he called out to them in a flamboyant manner, which exemplified his cheerful disposition. Seth thought: *It's the same ol' Chang I knew in Hong Kong.*

Chang continued to peddle quickly from the vicinity of central Chinatown to an isolated area known as the foreigner's cemetery, where only a few mourners were scattered across the grounds. He hopped off the bicycle and with a broad grin turned to Seth gushing with enthusiasm, "Holy catfish! I never thought you see me again. You always in big trouble. My greedy, no good scum Uncle Tso still make plenty trouble for you. Rachel in bad kettle of fish."

Seth's happiness at seeing Chang was short lived. His worry and stress over the past weeks reached the pinnacle of his worst fears for Rachel's safety and his emotions now teetered on panic realism. There was a moment when his sensibilities were numb, void of thought, as the shock took its toll. With a tight grip on Chang's arm Seth urgently asked, "You have to tell me what has happened to Rachel! How did I get involved? And what are we all doing in Japan?"

"Uncle Tso hide Rachel in Japan for safekeeping. He no want General Von to catch him while he smuggle opium out of Canton. He keep Rachel hostage long time as his free ticket to do bad things. Uncle Tso very bad man." Chang became silent for a moment as if filled with remorse; then he perked up with a whimsical renewed energy and continued, "But he very great man in War. He get many medals from President Chiang Kai-shek… even Emperor Hirohito honor him. He very great general." With a plunging slide of emotions and eyes focused on the ground, Chang mumbled in a low tone, "He go down hill fast after War and now he very, very bad man… but very *rich* bad man."

The two sat resting their back against a tombstone as Chang told his story.

CHAPTER TWENTY

It was early morning when Seth awoke. Noise from the street filtered into the small back room of a tailoring shop in Chinatown, which was provided by Chang's friend. This would now be his asylum for safety during the next few days or until he returned to Korea. For a few seconds, his thoughts reverted to a time in his youth when he would revel in the early morning hours to daydream mystical vignettes of his becoming a famous architect, traveling around the world to design beautiful buildings, which would be his legacy to mankind. These early morning hours were his time to daydream or to solve the problems facing a young man.

With his hands cupped under his head while he rested on the cot, his mind quickly conjured up all the critical details of Rachel's predicament as Chang had painstakingly told him. It seemed a lifetime away since his insouciant thoughts were happy and light hearted. A psychodynamic metamorphosis of his mental and emotional behavior took place in Korea escalating his maturity where his early morning thoughts were war related concentrating on survival. Of course, there were happy interludes when he envisioned spending the rest of his life with Rachel, but this brief happiness was quickly consumed by worry of her being held captive by General Tso.

Seth opened his eyes into a fixed stare while his mind raced with the words Chang spoke at the cemetery describing Rachel's kidnapping. His eyes filled with tears; his thoughts became morbid as the feeling of helplessness for her capture was overwhelming. He closed his eyes to concentrate… while going over in his mind Chang's story.

*****

Chang first explained he was born in Hong Kong on a floating junk in a fishing village in Aberdeen Harbor as was his father and his father's brother, Uncle Yen Tso. Shortly after Chang was born, his father moved his wife and children to Chinatown, Yokohama, as he did not want to be a fisherman like all the men in his family. He wanted to learn tailoring… hoping to raise the standard of living for his children. His father decided the best place to become a tailoring apprentice was in the large, ever-growing Chinese district in Yokohama. As a youngster, Chang played hide-and-seek in the crowded streets with many of the other children, thereby learning his way around Chinatown, which knowledge proved invaluable many times. Months before Japan invaded China, the family returned to Hong Kong and Chang's father joined the Chinese Army. He was killed very early in the war, leaving Chang and his siblings responsible for supporting the family. Seth thought, *well that explains how he knows the streets of Chinatown so well. And with deeper concern…Chang's role as a double agent is extremely dangerous. Uncle are not, General Tso is a formidable enemy and I feel certain he will have no compunction in handling any situation where Chang is involved… nephew or not. He will do whatever it takes to keep Rachel.*

Seth was surprised to learn that General Von Horstmann had so much clout in the Pentagon in Washington, D.C. Perhaps it was true as Chang had said in Hong Kong, "General Von like dynamo at power plant… much force."

Seth sat up in bed, contemplating the previous events of the last few days, and in bewilderment he shook his head wondering what the next few days will hold in store for him. His orders are to keep a low profile until Chang contacts him. *Each minute will be an hour.*

CHAPTER TWENTY-ONE

How many days has it been... or has it been weeks that I have been held a prisoner in this awful, moldy, smelly cell? Rachel questioned.

Her perception of reality is now vivid as her memory has completely returned, but the same old questions continue to taunt her. One day blends into the other as time drags slowly, depressing her mental disposition, and she starts marking the passing days on the cell wall. She considers herself fortunate, however, that she can climb onto her cot to look out the only window in her cell to the bustling harbor. She is persistent with trying to attract someone's attention by pounding on the window; but with the noise and activity in the whole wharf area, her efforts are to no avail.

A letter from Seth, which is tucked deeply in her trouser pocket underneath her tunic, helps to alleviate the grief of her predicament. By habit, she keeps Seth's most recent letter with her at all times to read and reread over and over again until she receives another letter to take its place in the trouser pocket. Then she carefully takes the older letter and places it with the others she has received, ties them all together with a blue ribbon and puts them in the nightstand by her bed. She considers herself very lucky that her captors did not search her.

Jeannine Dahlberg

She smiles to herself when reading Seth's letters for he constantly writes of his good fortune in finding her in a remote corner of the world. In sharing their love for each other through these letters, their desire to be together has intensified where it is no longer the distance in miles they regret, but the many hours of loneliness they must spend apart. Rachel retrieves the letter from her pocket… silently weeping. Her heart aches for Seth and she quietly whispers to herself as she has found that hearing her own voice is a comforting method in retaining her sanity. *I have taken this letter in and out of my pocket so often it's frayed.* She carefully fondles the letter stretching the corners from the many folds. *It is I who am the lucky one to have found you. I still feel the thrill of your arms wrapped around me, holding me tightly, keeping me safe from that monster, General Tso, when he tried to kidnap me in Macau. Oh, Seth, I need to feel your tower of strength, now. I'm so alone. Thank goodness I have this one letter, which gives me courage to face another day. I don't know how much longer I can take not knowing where I am, who is holding me a prisoner, or when… or if I will ever see you again.*

As she starts to read the letter, a tear drops onto the page, making reading impossible for her tear-filled eyes. She closes her eyes, mentally visualizing the words, which are memorized… and she begins:

"My darling, Rachel: *The guns are silent tonight, but the noise from the restless men in camp is deafening, and, yet, the commotion does not break my concentration in thinking of you. My love is a deep reservoir of emotions churning inside with anticipated fulfillment of my heart's desire. I love you so much. My reasoning is obscure in trying to understand the role destiny will play in bringing us together. This war has cast a sea of troubles upon my mind and soul and heart. Korea is so cold. The sting of the frigid air penetrates through every part of my body. My only salvation is clinging to tender, loving thoughts of you, which kindles a rush of adrenaline that keeps me warm. I close my eyes and see your beautiful face. If I could…"*

The earth trembles, the stone floor moves beneath Rachel's feet and she screams. Dust particles drift slowly from the ceiling blanketing the floor in a white powder. Seth's letter falls from her hands to the white floor and she quickly retrieves it, fondly wipes off the dust and places the letter securely in her pocket. Her eyes are wild with excitement and she pleads: *No, no! Not an earthquake.*

CHAPTER TWENTY-TWO

The flight from Panama to Tokyo was uneventful and smooth, which was of no consequence to General Yen Tso. Regardless of flight conditions, he does not like to fly. It is not from fear of flying; it is the discomfort, and sometimes extreme pain, he experiences from the pressure in his ears. He is susceptible to sinus headaches, which aggravate the problem and dull his senses, and he wants to have all his mental faculties when he has his meeting with Sun Lo regarding the transfer of Rachel to his custody.

For the past few weeks, General Tso dedicated his thoughts to planning a safe and successful deliverance of Rachel to his care in exchange for joining forces with Sun Lo in operating the largest opium smuggling ring in the whole south Pacific area. Together, they plotted to kidnap Rachel and hold her hostage for whatever length of time it took to amass an enormous fortune, believing General Von would not interfere with their illicit business dealings so long as Rachel was in their hands. Sun Lo was to receive half the shipment of opium for his role in keeping the girl locked up in one of his warehouses at the wharf in Yokohama, making certain she would not be harmed in any way. The deal was to be concluded quickly after the ship arrived in Yokohama from Canton with the opium.

They had worked together on a few illegal business ventures earlier in the year reaping a harvest of wealth; and believing their fortune could escalate sky-high, they were both enthusiastic to make their newly found friendship viable. General Yen Tso, Chinese, and Sun Lo, Japanese, were the epitome of evil for their devilish deeds. Both were molded from the same wicked clay. Together, they knew they could expand their field of operation to create a formidable business enterprise in the Orient and in the Middle East.

As the plane approached the island of Japan, General Tso realized for the first time agreeing to be a partner with Sun Lo was probably the worst mistake of his entire life. It was a partnership, which was carved during a weak moment, when his love of money and lust for power clouded a clear mind. He realized this newly found friendship was a facade masking centuries-old animosity between their two countries, which was a hatred that was taught and continued to fester like a boil lingering in its malicious poison. Only a few short years ago, they were vicious enemies in the Big War and no length of time could ever heal the bitter memories. General Tso now berated himself for forming this partnership as he knew it could never survive, and reprimanding himself thought: *It was a mistake an ordinary, common fool could make.*

With so many urgent thoughts running around in his head regarding the meeting with Sun Lo and in his rush to board the plane, General Tso forgot the medicine for his sinus headaches. As he stepped from the plane unto the tarmac, he cursed himself for neglecting to take care of his own physical well-being and he knew the first order of business would have to be to go to the hospital pharmacy in Tokyo to pick up his medication. The meeting with Sun Lo would have to wait.

*****

It was mid-morning when General Tso walked into the lobby of the army hospital in Tokyo. The medicine he needed for his sinus headaches was easily accessible from the pharmacy without prescription… and he would need some eardrops. He walked quickly to the counter at the information desk. He noticed the woman behind the counter was English and he hoped she would be able to understand what he wanted from the little bit of English he knew.

"Pharmacy, please, where is it?"

The woman lifted her head to respond. With a slight gasp and pointing the direction, replied, "Yes, it's down this hall and to the right of the elevator." Sydney could not believe her eyes. Standing before her was the old man she had seen in the café in Panama a year ago. It was General Yen Tso. She would never forget him. His imperially slim body and arrogant posture of an overbearing manner, plus the large white wide-brim Panama hat he wore, characterized the picture she remembered of this powerful man. At a closer glance, she realized this man was not as old as she had remembered as it was the deep wrinkles in his face, which betrayed him to be much older.

Sydney was anxious to relay this important information to General Von, but she knew the general was traveling by an old Chinese junk on the Pearl River and could not be reached. She would have to wait until she heard from him with further instructions. Her left eye started to twitch, as was a common occurrence when she became nervous and she rubbed it vigorously hoping to dissipate the irritant, but to no avail. Time was running out and something had to be done quickly to get Rachel out of the warehouse where she was being held captive. Now, with the presence of General Tso in Tokyo, Sydney realized the urgency for a plan of action was imminent and the situation demanded immediate action to capture Rachel... and she was not certain General Von had formalized a plan, as yet. Everything hinged upon General Von's assessment of the situation in Canton regarding the shipment of opium to Panama. She knew the general could do nothing to prevent the smuggling of opium or Rachel would be killed. With all these concerns running through her mind, Sydney believed her left eye was going to bounce out of its socket. Everything hinged on General Von's plan.

Sydney stood at the information desk nervously flipping her pencil on the counter while keeping a watchful eye down the corridor for General Tso to return to the lobby. Her body stiffened under the anxiety of keeping a close watch on the front door also, as Quan Lee was due any moment for a scheduled meeting with her. Their element of surprise would be ruined if General Tso saw Quan Lee in Tokyo.

The lobby had begun to fill with patients, many in wheelchairs or on crutches, and visitors, who looked bewildered as to where to find the correct room for their visit. Many visitors stopped at the receptionist's desk to ask directions. Sydney tried to be pleasant when she hurriedly answered their questions, but the visitors knew by her tone of voice she was irritated by the rush of people at the desk. This was her second day of learning the job; and between answering the phone in Japanese or English and assisting with the many varied questions asked by the people, she found things could get a little hectic.

Sydney quickly glanced down the corridor and saw General Tso walking towards the front door. He was swinging a large white hat in his one hand, and with the other hand he was vigorously rubbing his forehead as if it hurt before placing the hat on his head. She watched as he slowly walked through the lobby toward the front door and left the hospital.

It was only a few minutes later when Quan Lee briskly made his way through the crowded lobby and approached the receptionist's desk. Sydney acknowledged his presence with a nod of her head and called to an assistant to relieve her for a short, well-deserved break. The two quickly found a quiet nook behind a large pillar at the back of the lobby where they could talk.

Sydney urgently asked, "General Tso didn't see you, did he?"

"No," Quan Lee responded, "but it was a close one. I was crossing the street when I saw this man who was wearing a large white Panama hat get into a black limousine and I knew that had to be Yen Tso." Quan Lee reminisced with the thought, "Even when he was a kid, he liked to put on airs to do something or to wear something that would make him stand out from a crowd. He always liked attention. Knowing him as I do, he probably thinks the hat makes him look important. It's all for show. Now, the white hat has become his trademark." Quan Lee started to laugh, "I think it makes him look like a dandy. And he would be plenty mad if he knew what I thought." In a more sincere tone of voice, he continued, "Many times we wrestled together trying to convince one or the other as to who had the better idea about… whatever. At that time in our life, it didn't make any difference. We were just playing."

Quan Lee brightened with a broad grin on his face, looked around the large pillar to make certain no one could hear him and reported, "Sydney, General Von called me early this morning from Canton and you won't believe the good news. I had to ask him twice to repeat it before I could comprehend what he said. I believe the positive forces of feng shui are with us today."

He stopped momentarily to absorb this stroke of good luck, which seemed like an eternity to Sydney. Finally, she insisted, "Quan, don't make me wait any longer. What is the good news?" Sydney could not begin to control her left eye as Quan repeated General Von's message.

"General Von and Adam arrived in Canton late yesterday afternoon and only a few hundred feet away at the dock was the *Ladybug.*"

Sydney felt a ripple of exhilaration flow through her body as she eagerly listened to Quan relay the message.

"General Von made contact late last night with our good friend Captain Oscarson, who is still commanding the *Ladybug*... and it gets even better." Quan Lee's voice is now higher pitched with excitement and continues. "Captain Oscarson was approached by a representative of Sun Enterprises to inquire if the *Ladybug* could transport some barrels of rice from Canton to Yokohama. He agreed to handle the shipment, but secretly examined the contents of the barrels and discovered that opium is being smuggled inside. He told General Von he planned to turn the barrels over to the narcotic division of the port authorities in Yokohama."

Quan Lee rubbed his hands through his hair in a state of disbelief and emphatically said, "Sydney, can you believe the euphoric feeling General Von must have experienced upon hearing this information." Quan Lee paused at this point trying to envision the General's happiness and continued, "General Von told Captain Oscarson his purpose for being in Canton and he carefully outlined the urgent need for the opium to arrive safely in Yokohama in order to secure Rachel's rescue from General Tso and Sun Lo." In a more relaxed tone of voice, Quan continued, "General Von and Adam will arrive late tomorrow night in Yokohama aboard the *Ladybug.*"

Quan Lee tried to contain his emotions for he knew there where forces beyond his control that answered everyone's prayers for a safe plan to rescue Rachel. He felt drained from excitement and fell back against the pillar in disbelief.

"Oh, Quan. What great news! We will all be in Yokohama tomorrow." Sydney's left eye stopped dancing and for the first time in weeks, she felt her whole body relax. She knew General Von would come up with a good plan for his daughter's rescue. A small smile escaped her lips as she thought: *The pieces of the puzzle are starting to come together.*

CHAPTER TWENTY-THREE

Both men were rigid... devoid of flexibility and humbled by Mother Nature as tremors of involuntary shaking rushed through the crust of the earth. It was a small discrete movement, but both Yen Tso and Sun Lo had the same thought: *Could it be a precursor to a major seismic event? The timing was all wrong. The shipment of opium had not arrived from Canton and the girl had not been transferred to Panama.* They both were men who enjoyed being in complete control of any situation, and they had the power to enforce their will. They did not like the feeling of uncertainty or insecurity forced upon them by an act of Mother Nature, and the thought of a possible earthquake was disquieting.

Sun Lo's office at Sun Enterprises in Tokyo was richly decorated and quite comfortable, but both men felt an anxiety to end the meeting quickly. After a few minutes when the nervous tension abated, they continued the spirited discussion of details to bring their plans to fruition.

Sun Lo cautioned with a haughty, pundit attitude, "This is the third temblor to hit the area in the last few days. They are nothing of any magnitude; but I fear if the next quake is more powerful, we may be confronted with a tsunami, or harbor wave, which is caused by seismic movements in the ocean and can move chains of waves swiftly across water at a tremendous speed. These waves grow in height when they approach land and I fear they may damage my warehouses along the wharf again. We must move the girl to a safer location until you can take her to Panama."

General Tso sarcastically responded, "You don't have to preach to me about the power of tsunamis and the frequency of earthquakes in Japan. My grandmother was killed while visiting friends in Tokyo in 1923 when a quake and subsequent fire killed well over one hundred thousand people." In a lordly, authoritative voice he continued, "I plan to leave Yokohama immediately with Rachel and my half of the opium when the ship arrives from Canton and…"

Sun Lo interrupted and snidely remarked, "Well, general, if Mother Nature has her way, you may have to wait awhile before you can leave Japan. Hopefully, weather permitting, the ship will arrive from Canton some time late tomorrow night and then we can conclude our business."

Tension, fueled by acrimony, started to kindle, as attitudes flared to a dangerous pitch.

"What's the name of the ship that is transporting the opium?" Yen Tso asked.

"It has a funny name for a tramp steamer." Sun Lo scratched his head as if to try to remember the name and slowly said, *"Butterfly... Dragonfly...* no, no, it's the *Ladybug."*

"You fool! Not the *Ladybug!"* Yen Tso bellowed.

With glaring eyes and gritting his teeth while trying to control his temper, Sun Lo spoke softly and slowly, "There is no problem. My man in Canton thoroughly investigated both the captain and his cargo, and he reported the shipment of opium, which is buried in barrels of rice, will arrive in Yokohama along with other cargo being transported. And the good news is the *Ladybug* will sail immediately for Panama, which is its next stop. That sounds perfect to me." Sun Lo bristled with the thought of being called a fool and with a contemptuous attitude continued, "Your share of the opium can remain aboard ship and be transported to Panama… along with Rachel."

"And what is General von Horstmann doing all this time while we are easily sailing away with the opium? I can't believe he hasn't tried to rescue his daughter. It seems inconsistent with his normal stratagem to let us win so easily," Yen Tso queried and quickly asked, "Where is General von Horstmann, now? Did your man say?"

"He informed me the general arrived in Canton a couple of days ago to seek a safe deliverance of the opium to us. He wanted to handle this shipment personally, with no mix ups, in order to obtain his daughter's freedom. It appears even a general will tumble to defeat if the stakes are high enough." With a mean, evil laugh, Sun Lo growled, "He is under the influence of delusion if he believes we will set his daughter free;" and continued, "He and my informer are traveling together aboard the *Ladybug.*"

Sun Lo paused a moment and then demanded, "What do you know about the tramp steamer that I don't know?"

With alacrity, Yen Tso gave a complete account enumerating in detail how he had planned to smuggle Hitler's gold bullion aboard the tramp steamer, which sailed from Le Havre, France, through the Panama Canal to Hong Kong… replete with the confrontation with General von Horstmann's men aboard the *Ladybug* in Macau.

He smugly added, "It was a good plan, too, and it would have worked had I not used that quisling Andre to travel with the gold shipment aboard the *Ladybug.* He was a stupid fool."

Sun Lo responded, "It is very wise that you have your base of operation in Panama where you are tucked away safely from the authorities. I suppose you have never seen General von Horstmann or Captain Oscarson, who is the captain of the *Ladybug.*"

"That is correct, and that is why I feel quite safe to have come here to make final arrangements and to handle this operation, personally. In a few days, we will have the opium, and the girl will be in my custody. I am deeply annoyed, however, that once again the *Ladybug* is involved in one of my exploits. The *Ladybug* was not lucky for me before and I am concerned the positive forces of feng shui may not be with me."

Sun Lo roared with laughter and with a sarcastic lilt to his voice said, "Don't tell me a brilliant man like you is superstitious. You are a fool!"

Yen Tso jumped to his feet and grabbed Sun Lo by the neck pulling him up from his chair and snarled, "Don't you ever call me a fool!" With lightning thrust, Yen Tso hurled him back into his chair. Sun Lo sat dazed from the quick assault.

The office door partially opened to reveal the secretary standing in the doorway. She had heard the commotion and loud voices and glanced at Sun Lo slumped in his chair. She stood frozen for a few seconds under the glare of Yen Tso and was afraid to move.

With a quick stride from across the room, Yen Tso proudly marched to the door, placed his white Panama hat on his head and called back to Sun Lo, "The girl stays in the warehouse until the ship arrives. No one touches her."

Yen Tso was thoroughly agitated with the tone of the meeting and once again berated himself…thinking *it was absurd to think a friendship could blossom from the dust of ancestral hatred.*

The secretary waited a few moments until Yen Tso was out of sight and then rushed to assist Sun Lo, who was still coughing and gasping for breath.

Making a promise to himself, Sun Lo uttered, "Yen Tso will meet his ancestors shortly."

CHAPTER TWENTY-FOUR

"Where is he?" Rachel sobbed. Troubled and totally frustrated with her dangerous predicament and bleak existence, Rachel stared at the tiny etched marks on the concrete wall. Slowly, she runs her finger over each mark representing a number for the days she has languished in her cell, while painfully remembering that each day and longer night has brought no hope of deliverance from her captors.

Weakened by the decreasing vitality of living in a state of depression, her normally cheerful disposition gave way to listlessness. She counts eleven marks on the wall and carves one more as tears roll down her cheeks. She cries loudly, "Chang, where are you!"

Rachel's call echoed down the long hallway to the jailer's station. She could hear the heavy sound of leather boots on the stone floor resonating in the narrow corridor as the guard came running toward her cell. She sat on the floor with her back against the wall and braced herself for another clash with the man she has come to despise.

What the Japanese guard lacked in height, he made up in weight, being almost as round as he was tall. He was extremely cumbersome in size, bungling every movement his body made as if he had no control, and his thick glasses accentuated the problem with coordination. He was a very unhappy man, cursing his size and clumsiness, which contributed to his mean disposition.

He fumbled with the key at the door latch, and tried unsuccessfully to be swift in movement. Finally, the door opened and he scanned the cell with poorly focused eyes to find Rachel sitting on the stone floor. He had been given strict orders not to harm her in any way, but he followed these orders with disdain. As was his routine when entering her cell, he pranced back and forth in front of her with a lustful smirk, extending his arms as if he intended to grab her. He stroked her long hair and leaned closely over her.

Rachel remembered she had the knife hidden under her tunic and intended to use it if she felt in imminent danger. She was determined to put a stop to the guard's habit of his tauntingly offensive treatment. She stopped crying... fortified herself with strength, which came from heaven above... and with a defiant glare, she stared directly into the guard's eyes. His large, bulky body hanging threateningly over her was more than she could endure. She ripped his glasses from his face, kicked him hard in the groin and ran for the door. On hands and knees, the guard painfully crawled on the floor to find his glasses, which Rachel had thrown to the far dark corner of the cell.

Exhilarated with newly found freedom, Rachel ran out the door and down the long hallway. As she approached the guard's station, she noticed the corridor spider webbed into two more long halls leading in different directions. Her mind raced with thoughts of which corridor to choose that would lead her outdoors and away from the warehouse. Frantically, she chose the corridor, which was more brightly lit, and hurried to a door at the far end. Her heart was pounding as the rush of adrenalin carried her swiftly on legs that had not been exercised in many days. A feeling of happiness swept over her body as she pushed open the door to the glorious outside.

The crisp night air felt marvelous on her face as she looked upward to the star-studded sky, giving a prayer of thanks. The cool sea breeze and the fresh smell of the ocean made her feel alive. She closed her eyes, took a deep breath, lowered her head with a long sigh of relief and looked straight ahead to the harbor. Her happiness was short lived when her relaxed facial expression suddenly changed to one of horror with her eyes transfixed on a figure moving quickly toward her. Her knees went weak and she cried uncontrollably when she saw the relief guard, who was about thirty feet away, running toward her. He roughly grabbed her from behind as she tried to run. There was no way she could reach her knife to ward off his attack. Forcing her arms behind her and over her head, he dragged her into the warehouse while she was kicking and screaming for help. When they approached the long corridor, the guard keeper was stumbling out her cell moaning and bent over in a lot of pain. His eyes burned with hatred as he glared at Rachel while mumbling something inaudible in Japanese as the two passed at the threshold to her cell. With a quick, hard thrust, the relief guard roughly pushed Rachel into the dark, musty, smelly cell. She landed in a sprawled position on the cold stone floor... all hope abandoned. The huge steel door closed behind her with a reverberating sound that haunted her for the rest of the night.

Rachel's attempt to escape failed.

CHAPTER TWENTY-FIVE

It was a recurring dream that Seth had experienced many times over the last few months. Each time he would awake with the same thought: *It can't be a dream. I still feel the firm passionate touch of her lips on mine.* He brushes his finger tips lightly over his lips, feeling the thrill of love; and wanting Rachel so much his body quivers with the thought of making love to her.

The small room in the back of a tailoring shop, which Chang arranged with family friends in the Chinatown district of Yokohama was quite comfortable for Seth. The neutral wall colors with a few pieces of bamboo furniture, along with a futon for sleeping made the room the next best thing to being in his bedroom at home on the plantation. It far surpassed living in a tent in Korea listening to the sounds of war. There was a hibachi in the center of the room, which was used as a portable fireplace for keeping the room warm. A shoji screen was placed in the doorway between the tailoring shop and the small room, which created privacy for Seth while he was a guest.

At General Von's request, Chang asked the tailor to sew some street clothes for Seth to wear while in Japan on this assignment so he would not be recognized as an American army soldier. To add a touch of hospitality, the tailor made a kimono with an obis (or wide sash) as a special gift that was placed on the futon when Seth arrived. Seth quickly learned Japanese etiquette takes on a rigorously disciplined traditional form. The tailor and his wife were humbled to have an American guest from the army of occupation in their home and expressed their happiness with immense generosity. Fancy foods were prepared, Nippon beer was served and each day there was a special tea ceremony.

Seth also learned of the complexity of the Japanese culture. His hosts were gracious, and yet subservient in their mannerisms. They stressed external politeness to an extreme that embarrassed Seth in their desire to please. He wished he could experience this fine hospitality under happier circumstances. The heavy burden for Rachel's rescue was constantly on his mind.

His sleep had been disturbed by muffled voices in the tailoring shop. He recognized the one voice to be the tailor's; and the inflection in the other voice sounded a little familiar, but he was too engrossed in his own thoughts of Rachel, his dad and home to pay more attention.

Seth had not written a letter to his dad, BillyJoe, in four weeks and he knew his dad would be plenty worried if he did not hear from him soon. His dad's Saturday morning ritual was to write him a letter and Seth really looked forward to mail call as he knew he could always count on a letter from home. Seth visualized the early morning kitchen routine of his dad standing at the stove preparing his favorite egg omelet breakfast. He could almost smell the bacon frying and the coffee brewing. He missed home.

He rested on the futon with his eyes closed and his hands cupped underneath his head, while conjuring up all the details of the events leading up to his arrival in Yokohama. So much had happened in a relatively short period of time that his thoughts swirled with disbelief. He made a promise to himself that in the morning he would write a letter to his dad, explaining why he had not received a letter from Rachel approving the financial statement reports for the plantation's auditor. He tried to think of how he could tell his dad about Rachel's kidnapping and his hasty trip to Yokohama to help with her rescue without his dad breaking down completely with worry.

It was well past midnight when Seth's eyes opened wide upon hearing a quiet knock on the shoji screen. He was in a trance-like state between dreams and reality... unable to absorb the vision he saw standing in the doorway. He thought he was hallucinating when he quietly whispered, "Chang?"

"You come quick! We go see where Rachael hide in warehouse," Chang urged.

With lightning speed, Seth jumped up and dressed. There was no conversation between the two as they ran to the rickshaw parked at the entrance to the shop. Chang peddled with great speed through the early morning quiet streets of Chinatown to the fourth gate where there was a car waiting for them.

Chang parked the rickshaw at the nearby rickshaw stand and both ran to the car. Seth hurriedly folded his tall body into a very small car… carefully making room for Chang.

Seth recognized the driver of the car and excitedly said, "Quan Lee, I didn't expect to see you here!"

Quan Lee admitted, "I never thought you would want to return to the Orient after your last experience on the *Ladybug* in Macau. That was one of the most vicious skirmishes in my career in fighting off the gangsters of the Triad society."

All three men sat in the car as it rumbled along the dark street to the wharf area. Each man was deep in his own thoughts, conjuring up the gruesome details of that fight. They remembered how General von Horstmann outwitted his adversary General Yen Tso with his strategy that foiled the Triad's effort to confiscate the gold bullion from the ship's hold… and kidnap Rachel.

Quan Lee thought out loud, "I can't believe General Tso is trying to kidnap Rachel, again."

Seth asked Quan Lee, "Is there anyone else involved in Rachel's capture whom I know?"

"Yes. Sydney is in Tokyo masquerading as a receptionist at the army hospital. And, Seth, this is difficult to believe. We both saw General Tso in the hospital where he picked up medication. Fortunately, he did not see me." Quan Lee continued in a low, remorseful voice, "We were childhood friends." And stumbling with his words mumbled, "We know one another very well."

"I hope General Von has thought of a good plan to rescue Rachel." Seth injected and said, "That makes four of us to liberate Rachel… Sydney, Chang, you and me."

"Well, there will be five of us. General Von is very much involved in this plan. He definitely wanted to be an active participant in rescuing his daughter. He felt a small number of people involved would be more effective than using a larger force. I hope he is right."

"Where is General Von?" Seth asked.

Quan Lee reported the good news of General Von's trip to Canton and his meeting with Captain Oscarson aboard the *Ladybug*. He confided all the pertinent details as he knew them including the proposed arrival of the ship in Yokohama within the next day.

Seth never could have imagined that he would ever see Captain Oscarson again. He was Seth's mentor while sailing from Le Havre to Macau. His admiration and respect for the captain spilled over into every thought of that dangerously exciting voyage. The captain was a brilliant man... a walking encyclopedia, who brought a new dimension to Seth's life with his teachings. He was excited with the thought of seeing the captain again.

Quan Lee had no trouble in driving the distance to the warehouse as there were very few cars on the road, and no bicyclists, at two o'clock in the morning, but he gave close attention to steering the old car around the many potholes in the roads, which were in desperate need of repair. He was familiar with the Yokohama harbor area and with the help of Chang they located the warehouse where Rachel was held captive.

Chang pointed to a window in one of the warehouses. "Look, you see candle burn in window. Rachel hide there."

Chang's words were like fireworks exploding in Seth's ears. He thought his heart would burst with the thrill of knowing Rachel was a stone's throw away.

Quan Lee stopped the car a short distance from the warehouse and cautioned, "General Von wants us to canvass the immediate area around the warehouse so we can present a plan to him when he arrives. I think if we explore a two-block radius that will be sufficient for us to draw an accurate sketch in close proximity of what we will be facing when we free Rachel."

Seth eagerly volunteered to investigate the immediate area closest to Rachel's window and the three split into different directions.

Candle in the Window

Thankfully, there was no moon and the dim light from the corner lamp posts afforded very little light. The lap of the waves against the wharf wall cut the silence with a constant splashing sound and only an occasional bell from one of the many ships anchored in the harbor disturbed the quiet surroundings.

Seth approached the window with great caution... constantly looking all around, making certain there was no other person in view. He estimated the iron barred window in Rachel's cell to be at least twelve feet from the ground with no means of scaling the wall. He was greatly disappointed that he would not be able to talk with Rachel. He believed if he could just hear her voice and know that she is okay, he would feel much better. He shuffled his feet on the loose gravel beneath her window desperately trying to come up with a solution to solve his dilemma of wanting to see her. He picked up a few small pebbles and tossed them one at a time against the window hoping to wake her. The first toss was right on target and he waited a few minutes to see if Rachel would appear in the window.

Rachel was sprawled on the stone floor softly sobbing while listening to the two guards walk to their station at the end of the hall. She felt immobilized as every bone in her body felt too heavy to move.

She slightly lifted her head from the floor glancing to the lit candle in the window when she thought she heard something hit the windowpane, but gave it no further attention as she was totally dejected and too drained of emotions to move.

Seth was poised, ready to throw a few more pebbles against the window when he heard the warehouse door open and close. He quickly ran around the corner for safety... stopped and turned to see a very fat man leaving the warehouse, who Seth surmised was one of the guards. The man appeared to be disabled as his body was bent over at the waist while holding his hand low at his side as if he were in pain.

With a bolt, Seth suddenly jumped when Chang startled him from behind with a tap on the shoulder.

"You see fat man?" Chang questioned. "He guard Rachel. Now, other guard guard Rachel."

Quan Lee joined the two at the corner of the warehouse and advised they had better leave before more guards from adjoining warehouses change shifts. The three walked quickly toward the parked car.

After serious thought, Chang mentioned, "It better we steal Rachel when fat man on guard. He not move fast." And after closer scrutiny, added, "He look funny tonight… like he fall on face."

CHAPTER TWENTY-SIX

Sydney was an attractive woman in her late thirties and still quite slender... thanks to the war years when there was very little food to eat in Britain. There were a few young men who expressed their desire to pursue a relationship, but there was always a reason for her not wanting to continue past a friendship. In retrospect, there were times when she thought about her young adult life and wondered if she should have married, but these thoughts were quickly put aside. She had one true love when she was young and he was killed on Sword Beach, along with many other young men from the British 6th Airborne Division, during the Normandy invasion. She believed you find your soul mate only once in your life and that there never could be another man she could truly love.

World War II was the cruel teacher, which forced her to become a master at relying on her own cognizance for survival, which imbued her with an overwhelming desire to create a safer world. Lingering thoughts of the war years always stirred up bitter memories of the many nights she cried herself to sleep. She was devastated when her lover was killed; and after her parents were killed during one of Germany's Luftwaffe nightly bombing raids, she thought her life was over. A strong feeling of guilt for having survived the war when everyone she had ever loved was killed goaded her with the thought: *I have been spared so that I may help create a safer world.* It was a grandiose idea... and she was up to the challenge. She went through extensive training in the field of espionage and became fluent in five languages… always diligent in the pursuit of attaining her goal of excellent qualifications to satisfy the standards required by the British Secret Service.

Sydney's previous experience in surveillance work was always at the frontline of encounter where dangerous situations call for calm, steady nerves, which she could not always control. It was the combination of her intelligence and experience along with perseverance that proved her invaluable when confronting an adversary. She thrived on the thrill of a close chase.

On this assignment, however, she felt she was not an active player in executing the plan to free Rachel. She thought: *Here I sit in a hospital in Tokyo at a desk and Rachel is in a warehouse in Yokohama.* She rationalized: *Well, I guess it is important that I am stationed at a location where I can take phone calls from General Von and Quan Lee.*

Her work at the desk was quite demanding, which helped the hours pass quickly, but it was tedious work, which necessitated that she sit at a desk all day. She felt too confined and too far removed from the action.

She was engrossed with these thoughts when the phone rang startling her. She recognized the voice and cheerfully said, "Quan Lee, I was just thinking about you and wondering how everything went last night."

"Chang directed us right to the warehouse," and in a tone of amazement continued, "Rachel puts a candle in the window at night, which made it quite easy for us to locate her room. Chang said the guards are so stupid they probably don't know it's placed there as a signal for help."

"Did you make contact with Rachel?" Sydney urgently asked.

"Seth threw a couple of pebbles at the windowpane, but we had to run and hide when one of the guards came out the door. We are not certain if she looked out the window." And in a brighter tone, "We were able to determine the changing of the guard and we surveyed the surroundings. The three of us feel confident about our plan to rescue her. In fact, we would like to do it tonight, but we know we should wait for General Von to arrive."

"The *Ladybug* docks late tonight in Yokohama, right?" Sydney asked.

"Yes, and Sun Lo has asked Chang to check on Rachel tonight before the ship docks to make certain that she is okay before General Von arrives. Sun Lo wants a smooth transfer of Rachel in exchange for his half of the opium."

Sydney gasped, "Oh... he's back!"

"Who's back?" Quan Lee asked.

"General Yen Tso is slowly working his way through the crowded lobby. But this is strange, he is staring at me. I hope he doesn't remember me from our quick encounter in the café in Panama. We were seated in separate booths, but we had full vision of each other."

"Is he walking toward your desk?"

"No, thank goodness. He is walking down the hall toward the pharmacy."

"Yen Tso must have one of his migraine headaches if he had to come back for more medication." Quan Lee cautioned, "Be careful, Sydney, he has always had a good memory for names and faces."

"Quan, perhaps I should follow him when he leaves the hospital. If I can locate his base of operation and perhaps learn how many of his men will be involved, then I can report to General Von how big of a force he will be facing... if an encounter should take place." Sydney believed this reasoning was sound, and with enthusiasm thought: *then I will feel I am taking part in the action.*

"No! Don't do that!" Quan excitedly answered. "For all we know, Yen Tso may have one of his bodyguards following him at a safe distance, or even stationed in the hospital or wherever Yen Tso thinks he may frequent. He is a very cautious man... nothing escapes his pervasive scrutiny to avoid danger. He has managed many narrow escapes by remaining sharp in taking precaution."

Sydney's shoulders drooped as the rush of adrenalin plunged to a new low. She would be stuck at the desk for the remainder of this operation. Deep in her own thoughts, she said nothing and hung up the phone.

Quan Lee heard the click of the receiver... the line was dead. He hoped Sydney would heed his warning.

*****

Sydney performed her duties at the desk in a perfunctory manner. Her mood was sullen as she routinely assisted answering the visitors' questions while her eyes were constantly glancing at the wall clock. Finally, it was six o'clock and her shift ended. It had been two hours since Yen Tso entered the hospital and to Sydney's knowledge, he had not left. She became more nervous with each passing hour wondering what was detaining him longer in the hospital. She tried to be vigilant in her attention to watch for his return to the lobby, but thought: *maybe he slipped out the door when my back was turned.* She decided there was nothing to worry about, but the nervous twitch of her eye betrayed the calm mood she tried to assume, which irritated her mood even more. She said goodnight to her friends at the desk and left the hospital.

It rained a good portion of the late afternoon and she was thankful for the short walking distance to the boarding house where she was staying. Her concentration of thought was given to the difficulty of jumping over all the water puddles standing in the old crumbled concrete sidewalk. She was not happy living in the slum section of the city where derelicts and prostitutes made up ninety percent of the population; but for the short period of time she would be in Tokyo and considering the close proximity of the boarding house to the hospital, the room would suffice. She paid no attention to a man wearing a Panama hat walking a short distance behind her.

Lightening cracked across the night sky followed by loud bursts of thunder, and wind gusts blew the rain pelting the ground at an oblique angle. The neighborhood was quiet with everyone taking sanctuary from the storm indoors. Sydney gave no thought for her own safety while running through the streets, clutching her purse with one hand while trying to hold her coat collar over her head with the other hoping to keep her hair dry. Her first concern was for the safety of the *Ladybug*, which was scheduled to arrive in Yokohama harbor late that night bringing General von Horstmann. All the players to free Rachel from her captors were coming together and she dreaded the thought of a serious storm pounding the area.

She ran to her boarding house, jumping two steps at a time to the alcove of the doorway when with a strong pull on her shoulders her body was whirled around bringing her face to face with Yen

Tso. The surprise was overwhelming, which was reflected in her eyes. Yen Tso was swift while Sydney's reflexes were slow. Fear gripped her mind and body, holding her frozen and unable to react. All the training in the world could not have prepared her for this sudden assault. With her emotions frazzled from personal, irritating mental reflections she had harbored all day, she was totally taken off guard.

Evil eyes stared into hers and with a grimace Yen Tso muttered through clenched teeth, "I remember you from Panama... and the *Ladybug.*"

With his left hand he grabbed Sydney by the throat, holding her tightly as her eyelids fluttered. "It took two years of thorough planning to arrange to steal that gold bullion. I tracked that gold from Hitler's treasure trove from one European city to another... and you and General von Horstmann stopped me in Macau. That was my gold! Do you hear me? MY gold!"

Yen Tso's anger swelled uncontrollably. Swift of hand, he plunged a knife deep into Sydney's stomach. Smiling, as he looked down, he believed his murderous act was justified. He slowly withdrew the knife and threw Sydney's limp body in front of the doorway, muttering, *you're next General von Horstmann.*

There was no one around to attest to Yen Tso's heinous act as he left the alcove unnoticed and slowly descended the stairs. His smug, righteous attitude helped to diminish his anger while his taut muscles relaxed, and he knew once again his wicked deeds would go unpunished. As he left the shelter of the alcove, a strong gust of wind carried his white hat off his head and into a nearby tree... too high for him to reach up to get it. His hat had become more than a cover for his head; it was a symbol of good luck... a status piece of apparel that brought him respect. He was not happy to leave the hat in the tree, but he had no choice. The rain drenched his clothes as he quickly returned to the hospital where his black limousine awaited.

Sydney collapsed in the alcove on the old wooden floor dumbfounded with eyes wide open in shock of disbelief as to what had just happened. Blood trickled from her mouth; her eyelids fluttered, then closed... as life drained from her body.

CHAPTER TWENTY-SEVEN

The old tramp steamer *Ladybug* pulled into its birth in Yokohama early in the morning as Captain Oscarson decided to ride out the storm at sea rather than navigate the vessel into a crowded harbor during a rainstorm late at night.

The rising sun resembled a huge ball of fire at the horizon... where the sky and sea become one, with the sunrays painting a surreal canvas of color on the calm sea. The bright blue sky showed no signs of the dangerous storm the night before as the *Ladybug* gracefully slipped into its birth at the wharf.

As a young man, Captain Oscarson pursued a formal education at Lund University in Lund, Sweden, where his studies in liberal arts and theology enforced his knowledge as an erudite scholar. It was his love of the sea with its magnetic power, however, which allured him to follow in the tradition established by his grandfather at the turn of the century to be a third generation sea captain. It was not an easy profession to perpetuate as both world wars created a hardship on the family business when private shipping was almost non-existent. Sweden, however, was a neutral country during both wars; and with his business acumen and knowledge of sailing most all the seas in the world, he negotiated certain sea lanes where his ships could sail and the business survived; and in fact, it managed to grow under his command. He loved the sea and his small fleet of three ships, which traversed the sea lanes all around the world. His customers respected him for his honesty and dependability and his crewmen respected him for his fairness in providing a workable contract with wages and bonuses commensurate with duties performed.

It was a long night. Captain Oscarson and General von Horstmann were both happy to be on deck of the *Ladybug* admiring the beautiful sunrise while standing at the railing looking at the long row of warehouses, which faced the boardwalk. Most of the crewmen, including Adam, were still seasick and remained below deck. The storm had wreaked havoc on shore as many warehouses appeared to have suffered some damage from the wind. Both men stood quietly, side-by-side, while sipping their last cup of coffee. They both stared at the warehouses and were consumed with the same thought for Rachel's safety and hoped she was not a prisoner in one of the damaged warehouses.

"I have sailed through many storms, but that one last night was a real winner." Captain Oscarson declared. "Let's hope for good weather while we are in Yokohama."

"I agree!" General Von confirmed. "I always thought it was a rough ride on a horse when I was in the cavalry during World War I; then I thought riding in an armored tank in World War II was a rough ride, but nothing has compared to the ride we had last night. I never have seen waves that high."

"This old ship can take a lot of pounding… she's been a good old girl." Captain Oscarson lamented.

Both men fell silent again as they relived last night's experience.

The captain broke the silence, "You know, this part of the world is notorious for its tsunamis and most occur during this season of the year," and in his usual pundit style continued. "The epicenter can be hundreds of miles away sending shock waves traveling through the earth at great speed and within minutes these waves can begin jiggling sensitive equipment at monitoring stations around the world. There can be earth shooting up maybe ten to twenty feet or more, which produces underwater landslides. The ocean is angry and a tsunami is created. It's an underwater wave where its effects are apparent only when it reaches shore… often hundreds or even thousands of miles away. Many tsunamis have hit the shores of Japan."

Candle in the Window

General Von was distracted from the conversation when his attention was drawn to a lithe figure quickly running and hiding from one obstacle along the wharf to another as he made his way to the *Ladybug*. The general immediately recognized the figure and asked the captain to lower the gangplank so Chang could board the ship.

"Me come fast to tell you Sydney killed last night." Chang excitedly said as he ran up the gangplank.

"What? How do you know this?" General Von exploded.

"I stop by boarding house very late last night after storm hit. Quan Lee say he worry she follow my Uncle Yen Tso. I go to boarding house make sure she safe in house."

Chang paused for a moment trying to catch his breath and continued, "I get there, and place swarm with police like bees in hive. They think she killed for money. Purse, rings, shoes… all gone. They say she in wrong place at wrong time. It very bad neighborhood."

General Von and Captain Oscarson were shocked to hear the story and stood looking at Chang for some kind of an explanation. They did not want to believe that she was dead.

"I never should have asked her to take part in this rescue effort… and then to be a victim of a random killing for money… this is more than I can handle," General Von lamented.

"Maybe killed on purpose," Chang suggested. "I stand long time looking at police and people from boarding house standing around and I look up to see rising sun and big tree that catch white hat during storm." With a big grin on his face and a look of intelligence, Chang chirped, "That hat belong to Uncle Tso. He only one I know who wear big funny white hat."

"That bastard!" General Von yelled. "He is more cunning than I thought if he knew Sydney was working at the hospital. He didn't assume that it was just a coincidence that she was in Tokyo. He connected her presence with a plot to capture Rachel. He now knows I will try to rescue Rachel and that I will not give him the opium."

General Von stormed around the deck of the ship, swiftly swishing the riding crop he held in his hand back and forth, as if killing the air as he would like to kill Yen Tso.

"I go fast now. Sun Lo ask me to go to warehouse to see if Rachel safe so he give her to you when time come so he get his opium. Uncle Yen not see Sun Lo yet this morning. When they meet, they maybe make new plan and we not get Rachel." Chang ran down the gangplank.

General Von called to Chang, "Wait, take this riding crop with you and give it to Rachel. She knows it's mine and I hope it will lift her spirits."

Chang reached for the crop, "Okay boss. Me go fast."

Captain Oscarson and General Von watched as Chang zigzagged his way through the debris and obstacles on the boardwalk.

"Good heavens!" General Von declared. "With all the excitement about Sydney, I failed to ask Chang in which warehouse Rachel is being held captive. I don't believe it!" He grabbed his head with his hands in total frustration.

Captain Oscarson tried to calm General Von, "Let's wait here on deck and watch Chang to see where he goes."

"I'm going to kill General Tso with my bare hands… and I will enjoy it." General Von promised.

The two men watched until Chang entered one of the warehouses. They looked at one another, nodding their heads with pleasure in knowing where Rachel's cell is located.

General Von started to speak, "We must…"

He stopped in mid-sentence when he saw Adam come on deck and quickly changed his thought and continued to say to Captain Oscarson, "We must enjoy this beautiful morning."

Adam walked up to both men saying, "I'll agree to that. Boy, what a storm last night. I hope I find my sea legs; I don't ever want to be that sick again."

All three stood at the railing looking at the glorious color of the sun.

CHAPTER TWENTY-EIGHT

Chang stopped at the door to the warehouse; took a couple of deep breaths to gain his composure and slowly walked down the long hallway to the guard's station... twirling the riding crop in his hand like a baton. He could easily see by looking at Wang's face that he was agitated. The Japanese guard was sitting at the desk and glared at both men as they spoke in Chinese.

"What took you so long?" Wang asked.

"Why should you care," Chang offered. "You're not my boss." As if to flaunt the riding crop like a prize, Chang continued, "Isn't this a fancy stick I found. It must have washed down the hillside from one of those big houses during the heavy rain."

Wang motioned for the guard to get up and walk down the hallway to open Rachel's cell.

The guard was very slow to move and Chang volunteered his opinion to Wang in Pidgin English, "He sure walk funny... like bent tree in wind.

Wang said, "There you go again in that funny talk."

The Japanese guard opened the cell door wide to see Rachel standing by the window. He hobbled across the room to stand at her side and with a look of disgust and consumed with anger, he muttered, "You, bitch! If you stay here much longer, you may just get hurt."

Rachel must have read his mind and backed away from him. She did not understand the language, but she knew what he was thinking.

Rachel glanced from Wang to Chang as they entered the room and was happy to see the guard leave. Wang approached Rachel with a lustful glimmer in his eye… and Rachel thought, *not again*.

Chang pushed Wang aside and started twirling the riding crop as if to show off his talent. He strutted around the cell for a few seconds, hoping Rachel would recognize the riding crop and then offered it to her so she could try her skill at twirling the crop. Rachel grabbed the crop quickly and with both hands fondled it as if it were a great treasure. She started to cry… they were tears of happiness. She knew it belonged to her father.

Wang took the crop from her hands and gave it to Chang. "What's going on; does she think we are going to beat her with it? She's crying like a baby already and we haven't touched her." And in a disgusted tone said, "Come on, Chang, let's go. She looks fine to me. I'll be glad when she's out of here… and I'll be glad when I'm out of Japan."

Wang was in a hurry to leave the cell and left immediately. Chang lingered a few seconds longer to talk to Rachel, "You wait, see. Not to worry. Number one plan work… soon."

More tears of joy streamed down her cheeks. She knew her father had to be in Yokohama somewhere in order to give the riding crop to Chang. The word, "soon" rang in her ears like church bells in a steeple… what a glorious sound. She climbed on top the bed railing so she could look outside to the harbor. The sun was brilliantly shining on a new day, and she felt rejuvenated with a new life, which she attributed to the riding crop she had held in her hands. She absorbed her father's strength from the crop, like young blooms receive the morning dew, and she thought, *what a spectacular day!*

CHAPTER TWENTY-NINE

By mid-morning, activity on the boardwalk had increased tenfold. Longshoremen and sailors were busy loading and unloading cargo from the many ships, which work had been disrupted by yesterday's afternoon storm. Yokohama was one of the most famous port cities in the world and the morning activity reflected its importance. The *Ladybug* rested at the wharf alongside great shipping vessels from many countries. True, the *Ladybug* is an old tramp steamer, but her fine reputation follows her into every port; and Captain Oscarson makes it a point to know, personally, all the authorities in every port where his ship docks.

Captain Oscarson and General Von worked tediously on a plan to rescue Rachel while sailing from Canton to Japan. They meticulously went over every detail with regard to handling the transfer of the barrels of rice, which carried the opium.

It was important that the ship remain docked at the wharf for as long a time as was needed to rescue Rachel. With this purpose in mind, Captain Oscarson initiated the first plan of action by contacting the port authorities immediately upon docking in Yokohama. He requested that the ship's cargo not be unloaded until an English speaking doctor from the army hospital in Tokyo could come to examine one of the deckhands who had become very ill. He politely suggested to the authorities he wanted to take precaution against the possibility of spreading a communicable disease to the people of Yokohoma… for which the port authorities thanked him for his consideration.

At the time when this first plan of action was decided, General Von and Captain Oscarson did not know that Sydney had been killed. Their idea of having the *Ladybug* placed under quarantine now presented a new problem involving the ability to communicate with Quan Lee. All messages had previously gone through Sydney while she worked as a receptionist at the hospital. General Von realized his only alternative was to involve the police captain in Chinatown. Over the years, Quan Lee and the police captain often worked together on drug related incidents involving Hong Kong, and they had become good friends. General Von felt confident he could rely on the police captain for assistance.

Captain Oscarson and General Von remained on deck for a couple of hours awaiting the arrival of the doctor, while marveling at all the activity on shore. Of particular interest, was the number of men milling around the warehouse where Rachel is held.

Adam paced back and forth on deck, leaning over the railing periodically as if he were waiting for someone from shore to contact him. With the new problem of the ship possibly being put under quarantine, he was concerned that he may not be able to go ashore. He had devised a plan of his own. He knew he was in a dangerous predicament by playing on both sides and he wanted to get as far away from both General Von and Sun Lo as possible. Once he collected his well-deserved money from Sun Lo for his role in kidnapping Rachel, he intended to hide for awhile in Japan. He was very pleased with himself for his shrewdness in outwitting General Von, but he worried if his good luck would continue now that there may be a delay in leaving the ship.

He stopped pacing, rested both elbows on the railing, started fidgeting with his hands and stared at the long row of run-down warehouses on the boardwalk. His thoughts turned to Rachel. A soft smile passed his lips and with a hint of evil reflected in his eyes, he thought: *I hope you are as miserable as you made me. I only hate myself for still loving you.* A nervous reaction to his thoughts, prompted him to start biting his fingernails. His concentration was broken when he felt a heavy hand on his shoulder.

"Well, Adam, you have the look of a man who wishes he were somewhere else?" General Von suggested.

"Well, it's for sure I wish I had a cigarette." Adam stated and continued, "Do you think I could go ashore to pick up a pack. I don't know if my fingernails can take more punishment."

"We are waiting for a doctor to come onboard to examine one of the deckhands… and if the ship is quarantined, we may be stuck in this harbor for awhile with no one being allowed to leave the ship. I'll be happy when this whole mess is over and Rachel and I can go back home." General Von asserted.

General Von knew Adam was waiting for one of Sun Lo's men to contact him with further instructions and he intended to keep Adam on the ship at all costs.

The sound of screeching brakes interrupted their conversation and they both turned their attention to an old car, which stopped close to the ship. A young man holding a black satchel got out of the car and hurriedly walked up the gangplank. It was the doctor.

*****

The ship's crewmen were all on deck waiting for instructions from Captain Oscarson regarding the transfer of the cargo. Most of them were over their seasickness and were anxious to get to work… not that they enjoyed working with the cargo, but they looked forward to the few hours of shore leave after their duties were finished while the ship was in port, which practice was customarily established by the master of the ship. The sailors were well aware of the rumor that had circulated regarding one of the new crewmen who was sick. He had come aboard as a new deckhand and no one had seen the sailor since the ship left Canton. Rumors ran rampant regarding the new sailor's identity and why he was sequestered in a private passenger room below deck.

Usually, the crewmen were busy with many chores, which were necessary in maintaining the ship; but this morning, the work schedule of unloading the cargo was on hold pending the doctor's diagnosis of the patient. The crewmen did not relish the idea of being confined to the ship while in port for an indefinite period of time, which would probably necessitate a task they hated... chipping and painting. Their irritable mood swings were becoming surly with each supposition, but the ripple of conversation ended when they stood silently watching the doctor board the ship.

Captain Oscarson greeted the United States Army doctor and quickly escorted him to the bridge at the center of the ship where they could have a private conversation with General Von. He moved some navigational charts from his desk; offered coffee, which was refused, and the three sat quietly for a few seconds. The doctor was a little bewildered that he would be asked to sit and drink coffee when he assumed he would be taken to the patient immediately.

General Von cleared his throat and said, "I think it is important that you know who we are, why we are in Yokohama and what our purpose is in calling upon you for your services."

The young doctor looked concerned as he did not know what to expect. His first thought was for his own safety. He did not know these men... were they honest... was he going to be shanghaied and forced to sail with the ship to foreign ports. His body stiffened as if he were preparing for whatever may happen if he should need to defend himself and he started to squirm in his chair.

General Von and Captain Oscarson took turns carefully outlining their credentials and giving an overview of their family history as was pertinent for the young doctor to know in order to satisfy the doctor's apprehension. The personal information was quite lengthy and impressive, which enforced their honesty and integrity as gentlemen.

General Von looked squarely into the doctor's eyes as if to siphon out his honesty through his eyes and continued, "I want you to swear an oath of secrecy that you will not divulge any information to anyone regarding the story you are about to hear."

The doctor was positively influenced by each one's autobiography. He relaxed and sat back in his chair to listen.

With alacrity, the general told the complete story of how Rachel was taken hostage in Hong Kong and was held in Japan to ensure a safe shipment of opium from Canton to Yokohama aboard the *Ladybug*. He expressed the urgency that his daughter must be released from her captors first; and if circumstances were in their favor, the shipment of opium would never be turned over to Sun Lo and General Yen Tso.

General Von choked out their names again, "Sun Lo and General Yen Tso are the two most unscrupulous men in all of Asia: murderers, thieves, extortionists, every vile vice you can imagine.... They will stop at nothing to get what they want and they will get it by whatever evil means it will take."

The three fell silent after the long story... each one was absorbed in his own thoughts. The doctor wondered where he was going to fit into this rescue effort and decided to ask the question.

"How am I going to help you rescue Rachel?"

Captain Oscarson responded, "We need a little time to get our people together and this is where we want you to buy some time for us."

General Von inserted, "When we were in Canton, we hired a sailor to come on board and sail with us to Yokohama. We told him that he would be paid handsomely if he would do what we wanted with no questions asked... and he agreed. He remained in his cabin for the entire voyage. We supplied him with theatrical makeup so he would look sick when the galley cook brought him his meals, and he was to show great difficulty in breathing. The sailor must be a good actor because the cook has announced his poor condition to everyone on ship."

"We need to have the ship placed in quarantine for a couple of days while our people get in place for the rescue," Captain Oscarson suggested. "And we also need you to ask the police captain in Chinatown to tell you where Quan Lee is staying while in Chinatown. This information, we want you to give to us, and it is important that we have this information as soon as possible.

The doctor agreed to help and suggested that he now take a look at the patient.

*****

The crewmen had no idea why the three men had to talk for a long time before the doctor was allowed to see the patient. They were concerned that the patient did, in fact, have a communicable disease and now, perhaps, their own lives were at stake. Rumors circled the ship at great speed as they awaited news of the doctor's report.

The doctor returned to the bridge where General Von and Captain Oscarson stood at the railing by the gangplank awaiting the results of the examination. In clear view of all the crewmen, the doctor reported that the sailor was, in deed, a very sick man. He had a high temperature, muscle aches, and great difficulty in breathing. He was reminded of a recent influenza epidemic in Japan when an acute febrile respiratory illness caused many deaths, which he said was an antigenic variant of influenza type A. He took throat cultures and blood samples and said he would report his findings as soon as the tests were finished. The doctor left the ship with all eyes on him. The crewmen appeared restless, but General Von and Captain Oscarson felt relieved that their plan was put into motion.

CHAPTER THIRTY

The radio room was rather antiquated with old communication equipment, but it sufficed for the needs of the *Ladybug*. The seaman in charge of receiving and dispatching messages was quite capable and managed to keep the equipment in good repair. It was a rather lonesome job, however, as there were never many cables that had to be sent and very few were ever received.

It was early evening when the seaman received a cable from the doctor at the army hospital in Tokyo. He was excited when he read the message and quickly rushed to the top deck where Captain Oscarson and General Von stood watching the activity on shore. The seaman was breathless from running the length of the ship, which caused the deckhands to take notice. Captain Oscarson grabbed the cable from the seaman and read the doctor's message to General Von: "Tests not complete. Have asked Doctor Quan Lee to take another vile of blood from patient. Have requested port authorities post a quarantine sign on *Ladybug*. The authorities demand you must sail out to sea to wait for test results. You must leave port by midnight tonight. I will cable you with diagnosis as soon as all tests are completed."

A few of the deckhands, who were standing close-by, became visibly agitated when they strained to hear the message being read, but heard nothing. The sharp sound of a hammer on nails brought everyone to the ship's railing. A longshoreman was nailing a quarantine sign on the gangplank.

Most of the sailors left the deck to return to their quarters below to continue playing cards. They were bored with their pathetic circumstance and impatiently waited to hear what the captain would have to say about their predicament.

Captain Oscarson and General Von continued to stay on deck giving vigilance to watching the men mingling outside the warehouse where Rachel is confined. They both wondered what, if any, action Yen Tso would take upon hearing about the ship's quarantine. Would he relocate Rachel? They believed and hoped that Rachel would remain safe if she continued to stay in the warehouse. For now, that is all they can do… is hope.

Long rays from the setting sun painted streamers of color on the harbor casting weird shadows of the ships onto the shore. Both men were becoming anxious to hear from "doctor" Quan Lee as time passed slowly from one long hour to another hour. Longshoremen were finishing their duties and sailors from other ships were returning to their respective vessels. Activity on the wharf was slowing down with only a few men lingering to talk.

A lone figure sprung from the deep shadows on shore and made his way to the *Ladybug*. Both men tried to hide their enthusiasm at seeing Quan Lee, who looked quite impressive masquerading as a doctor. He held a black duffel bag in his hand as he walked the gangplank.

"Gentlemen, I'm Doctor Quan Lee and I have been asked to see one of your deckhands to give him another examination." Quan Lee volunteered.

For the benefit of the few deckhands on deck, both men introduced themselves and walked to the bridge where they could talk. The three sat at the desk and Quan Lee quickly and quietly reported on the events of the day after the army doctor left the ship.

"The army doctor contacted the police chief in Chinatown, who in turn contacted me with the details of the doctor's meeting with you early this morning. I immediately suggested I masquerade as a doctor and return to the ship so I could personally talk with you regarding our plans." Quan Lee stopped talking and reached into the duffel bag to pull out a black shirt and black hood, which he handed to General Von. He continued, "I asked Chang's tailor friend to sew a black shirt and black hood for everyone who will be involved in rescuing Rachel."

Quan Lee looked around the bridge making certain no one could hear and he continued, "Seth is ready and waiting for orders." He turned to General Von and said, "Chang saw Rachel this morning in her cell and she knows you are here. And he told me to tell you that she looks fine." He hesitated a moment... then continued, "Our plan is to get Rachel out of the warehouse shortly after midnight and before the changing of the guard. Chang insists it is important that we rescue her at that time."

Both Captain Oscarson and General Von gave full attention to the plan as Quan Lee outlined. "General Von, sir, we want you to put on the clothing I just gave you and leave the *Ladybug* after dark tonight. I will be waiting for you at the end of the first row of warehouses. I will park my old car in the shadows and will flash my lights twice. We will then join Seth, who will be waiting for us in the shadows behind Rachel's warehouse. There is only one guard inside; and perhaps you noticed, the men who were standing around outside the warehouse were pulled off duty or they left on their own accord late this afternoon. We believe they were scared off by the quarantine sign."

Captain Oscarson repeated the information to Quan Lee about the necessity to sail the *Ladybug* out to sea by midnight as demanded by the port authorities.

All three men agreed this was a good idea. There was no way Yen Tso and Sun Lo could get the opium if the ship were at sea... if their plan happened to fail. Captain Oscarson suggested that he would call a meeting of all hands at nine o'clock, which meeting would be held below deck in the ship's galley. He would inform the men of the current situation regarding the ailment of the new deckhand and the purpose of the quarantine. This would allow General Von to slip off the ship to meet Quan Lee.

After a short examination of the sick seaman, Quan Lee returned on deck to bid good-bye to Captain Oscarson and General Von. For the benefit of the few crewmen on deck, his serious expression and quiet whisper gave the impression the seaman was, in deed, very ill.

CHAPTER THIRTY-ONE

The secretary was startled when she was interrupted by the sound of the office door being pushed with great force on its hinges as it swung hard against her desk. She jumped out of her chair and looked into the eyes of a frightful man with a sanguine complexion. She did not recognize him at first. It was his tall, slim body and large strong hands coupled with his bold, haughty demeanor that she remembered. She stood frozen; afraid to move. It was Yen Tso minus his large white Panama hat who stormed into Sun Lo's office looking mean and angry.

"We have a problem!" Yen Tso yelled.

"Oh, really? Just one? I can think of at least three problems," Sun Lo responded with a hostile attitude.

"I have reason to believe General von Horstmann has some of his agents stationed here in Tokyo." And with a slow, snide remark added, "If he thinks he can save both the girl and the opium, he is deluding himself."

"How did you find out about the agents in Tokyo," Sun Lo asked.

"Because I killed one of them last night and I know she wouldn't be here by herself. You do have your men guarding the warehouse where the girl is... right?"

Sun Lo turned his head to look out the window as he did not want to face Yen Tso and muttered, "They were there this morning, but they all left late this afternoon."

"What?" Yen Tso was livid with anger. "You fool! You let your men walk away?"

"There was nothing I could do. They were all afraid when they read the quarantine sign posted on the *Ladybug*. The flu epidemic that circled Japan a couple of years ago is still quite vivid in their memory and most of those men had grandparents who died in the great influenza pandemic in 1918. We all have heard the gruesome stories of the disease wiping out whole families. But don't concern yourself with my men. I will handle the situation in my own thorough way."

Yen Tso cleared his throat to spit on the floor, showing disgust. "Your men are a bunch of pansies."

Sun Lo studied Yen Tso with a cold, icy stare... not knowing whether to kill him now or wait until after he gets his share of the opium. The room was filled with hatred as the two stood silently... face to face. The word "fool" pierced his soul like a sword. He had heard it once too often and thought: *Be careful, Yen Tso. You may have to die today.*

Yen Tso tried to contain his anger and sarcastically said, "Well, I guess you had better tell me how this quarantine problem evolved."

"As I get the story, one of the deckhands may have a communicable disease and the doctor thinks it may be influenza. He is running tests now." Sun Lo almost stuttered when he reported, "The real problem is that the captain of the *Ladybug* has been told by port authorities that the ship must leave the harbor area until the tests are completed and something definite is known about the sailor's ailment."

"Do you mean MY shipment of opium is going to float around somewhere out there in the ocean while we sit here and watch the girl. How do you know this?"

"One of my men works for the port authorities... and that is OUR shipment of opium," Sun Lo demanded.

Yen Tso could no longer control his temper and snarled, "I knew the *Ladybug* was bad luck, and you have been bad luck for me from the beginning." He grabbed Sun Lo by the throat with his large strong hand and threw him on his back on top of the desk. Sun Lo gazed into Yen Tso's wild, wide eyes while his fingers frantically fumbled through the many papers lying on the desk feeling for the sharp letter opener. With one quick movement, Yen Tso pulled his knife from its sheath under his coat and thrust it into Sun Lo. "And that, my friend, ends a partnership that never should have begun. Now, you have no problems. The opium is all mine!"

The secretary heard the scuffle from the outer office and quickly hid under her desk. Her breathing was fast and heavy so she held her breath for fear of being discovered as Yen Tso stormed out of the office. She waited for a period of time, which seemed like an eternity, before she dared to come out from hiding. She gingerly tiptoed into Sun Lo's office almost afraid to see what she may find. Sun Lo's body had fallen from the desk into a crumpled heap on the floor. He was dead.

CHAPTER THIRTY-TWO

A black limousine was waiting at the curb for Yen Tso. He gave a few brief instructions to the chauffeur/bodyguard that he be driven to the Yokohama warehouse district at the wharf. He wanted to see for himself, firsthand, the location of the warehouse where Rachel was being held captive and to see where the *Ladybug* was docked. He knew his blood pressure was sky high as he could feel the red heat of his face, while his temples pounded as the migraine headache reached its pinnacle of pain. He settled back in the limo seat, poured a small glass of sake from the well-stocked liquor chest in the limo and tried to calm his nerves. He needed to think of happier times.

Scenes of his youth flashed before him as he would often think of the fun he had as a young boy playing with Quan Lee. Those were happy days when he did not know how very poor he was and the miserable life he had living on a boat in the fishing village of Aberdeen.

The war years contributed to educating Yen Tso to the realization that there was a better life after Aberdeen. His rise in the military to a general afforded him the benefit of a richer lifestyle and he was determined to be rich for the rest of his life. He vowed he would never again live in Aberdeen as a fisherman with the smell of fish always on his hands. And he enforced this decision by not being concerned with the means by which he would obtain his wealth as he believed the end resulting in wealth justified his method of obtaining it. He became angry when irritating thoughts kept popping into his head and he realized this was not the time to be happy.

When he arrived in Tokyo, he harbored many doubts about the whole idea of this operation ending in success. One looming concern was his consummating the partnership with Sun Lo, which he handled quickly to his satisfaction. The most important concern, though, was keeping the girl in order to ensure future successful drug hoists without interference from General von Horstmann and the narcotics bureau. All his energy and resources would be directed to keeping the girl.

He had been in Tokyo only two days and already he had killed two people. He could not believe that everything was going wrong so fast. His thoughts turned to Sun Lo: *I knew the negative forces of feng shui would be against me as soon as I agreed to become a partner with him. Of all the freighters in the world, Sun Lo selected the old tramp steamer "Ladybug" to transfer the opium from Canton to Yokohama. The "Ladybug" and I go back a long way.*

Once again, he tried to stop the tormenting thoughts to clear his mind from worry. His head pounded with a severe migraine headache and he tried to dissipate the pain by rubbing his forehead. His eyeballs ached in their sockets making his vision blurred. He swallowed a couple of sips of sake to relax, but he continued his disturbing thoughts: *General von Horstmann is my real problem and he is on the "Ladybug". If I were the general, I would try to get the girl tonight... before the ship has to return to sea. Wait! No! He is quarantined on the ship and he is not allowed to disembark.* He brightened with the thought: *Perhaps, the positive forces are starting to swing in my favor. I will take over Sun Lo's operation in Japan and handle it from my headquarters in Panama. I will move the girl to another location tonight... now that Sun Lo is dead. I will wait for the quarantine to be lifted and then I will make my move to get the opium... and I will make certain I keep the girl.*

The drive from Tokyo to Yokohama was not long and the time passed quickly as Yen Tso formed the plan of action, which he believed to be fail-safe. He was rejuvenated with happiness feeling he was in complete control again with Sun Lo out of the picture.

Upon Yen Tso's order, the chauffeur slowly cruised around the warehouse area and the immediate environs. It was early evening and the *Ladybug* was still docked at the wharf. He remembered Sun Lo telling him the ship had to be out of the harbor by midnight. There were a few men at the wharf close by the *Ladybug* who were carrying food and other necessities and placing them near the gangplank. Yen Tso presumed the ship would sail after taking on supplies. He read the big quarantine sign with interest: *This quarantine will work to my advantage. General von Horstmann will be anxious to get off the ship after a week or so at sea. He will want to end this deal as quickly as possible to get his daughter and he will gladly turn over the opium to me.*

For the first time in many days, a big smile brightened his face: *The opium is mine... all mine! None of it will have to be unloaded in Yokohama... Sun Lo is dead. The "Ladybug" is already scheduled to sail for its next port of delivery, which is Panama. Oh, how beautiful! It's going to sail immediately to my headquarters.*

Yen Tso took a small notebook from his coat pocket to sketch the general layout of the warehouses. After he was satisfied with the sketch and after studying the area, he realized he would need only a few men to help him transfer Rachel to another location. Some place where Sun Lo's men would not know where to find her. He told the chauffeur to return to Tokyo... it was time to talk to Sun Lo's secretary.

*****

The limousine turned into the business district in Tokyo where Sun Lo had his office. The street was crawling with policemen. Yen Tso surmised they were investigating the "horrible" murder of Sun Lo. He would have to wait to talk to the secretary and asked the chauffeur to drive him to the army hospital as he hoped to find out if General von Horstmann had more agents stationed in the area. He would return within an hour to Sun Lo's office when he thought the policemen would be gone.

Yen Tso pranced up the steps into the hospital as if he were a man in complete control of all situations. The item that was missing to carry off his arrogant posture was his white Panama hat, which he regretted. He walked straight to the receptionist's desk, choosing a Chinese woman to ask, "Could you please tell me where the nice British woman is today... the one who assisted me yesterday?"

The Chinese woman responded, "Oh, sir, I'm sorry to have to tell you that she was murdered last night."

Yen Tso tried to look shocked and continued, "Did she have family in Tokyo or was there anyone who came to visit her on occasion?"

"I can't answer that question as she worked here at the hospital for only a few days. I know of no one who came just to visit with her."

Yen Tso smiled; said thank you and returned to the limousine. With duplicity of thought, he wanted to believe that somehow she would have been involved in this operation and that she would have been contacted by someone with instructions... otherwise, she was a victim by association. It was imperative that he talk to Sun Lo's secretary as he had no further leads to follow.

*****

Timing was perfect. The policemen were leaving Sun Lo's office when Yen Tso returned. The chauffeur had not turned off the motor, when he flew out the door, held his head down as he brushed past the last officer on the stairway and rushed into the secretary's office. He wanted to talk to her before she left for the evening.

The secretary remained late at the office to assist the policemen with their investigation. She was very vague with her description of the assailant and was little help in describing the short altercation between the two men. In fact, her testimony became a figment of her imagination, as she did not want to be a reliable witness. She feared Yen Tso and did not want to be his next victim.

The secretarial position paid very well and for this reason the secretary was willing to look the other way when certain unlawful matters came across her desk. She never questioned nor pursued the reasoning behind any illegal methods of conducting business, and

Candle in the Window

for this reason Sun Lo compensated her loyalty generously for not discussing business outside the office.

Yen Tso quietly entered the office and stood at her desk for a few seconds before she turned from the filing cabinet and saw him. Yen Tso was pleased to see a look of fear sweep across her face. He thought: *I'm glad she's afraid of me. Perhaps, I will get the information I want right away.*

The secretary cried, "I didn't tell the police anything! Honest!" She thought: *Why did the police have to leave so quickly after the investigation. The man they want is right here.*

With a sinister smirk on his face, Yen Tso questioned, "What will it take for you to give me some names and addresses? Who are the men who check on the girl in the warehouse in Yokohama, who is Sun Lo's agent aboard the *Ladybug*, who works for the port authority, and where are Sun Lo's lieutenants?" He added, "You can do this an easy way by cooperating or I can get the information from you in a hurtful way. The choice is yours."

The secretary stumbled over her chair as she hurried to the rolodex on her desk. Her fingers were all thumbs as she tried to control her shaking hands while picking through all the cards on file. It took several minutes to find them as her extreme nervousness slowed her agility. After what seemed an eternity, she handed the cards to Yen Tso.

"Good!" Yen Tso gloated. "I have the cards... now, where are his lieutenants?" He yelled!

"They are in Panama waiting for the *Ladybug* to arrive. Sun Lo was never going to let you keep the other half of the opium shipment and he definitely was not going to let you keep the girl," she frantically said.

He stepped within inches of her and quietly whispered, "You're a good girl." And with one strong hand, he grabbed her by the throat. "I would hate to see something happen to you if you breathe a word of this to anyone," and he threw her into the chair.

Yen Tso gave her one last long look as if trying to decide if he should kill her, then slowly turned and left the office to return to the limousine.

The secretary fainted.

CHAPTER THIRTY-THREE

"I need a hat!" Yen Tso barked at the chauffeur as the limo made its way through the crowded shopping district of Chinatown. Yen Tso thought wearing a hat made him look more distinguished, but the real purpose was that he believed it brought him good luck. It was imperative that he buy a white Panama hat before he went to the warehouse to transfer the girl to another location. He wanted "lady luck" to ride with him.

Some shopkeepers had already closed for the evening. He became exceedingly nervous as he continued to yell to the chauffeur to find a hat shop that was open. The limo screeched to a stop in time to see the owner locking the front door. Yen Tso hopped out, and with a forceful grip on the owner's arm, persuaded him to open the shop.

Yen Tso returned to the limo with a smile on his face holding a big white Panama hat while the shop owner, visibly shaking, locked the door.

With the hat on his head, Yen Tso assumed a striking posture in the backseat of the limo with a facial expression, which exuded an air of confidence. He calmly poured a small glass of sake, puffed on a fat cigar and was now ready to proceed in trying to locate Wang and Chang in Chinatown. The card he procured from Sun Lo's office indicated that both men were coolies, working from the same rickshaw stand outside the fourth entrance gate to Chinatown. He slowly read the other address cards… Adam was on the *Ladybug* and not available and there was no need to contact Sun Lo's agent at the port authority. Yen Tso believed that with the help of Wang, Chang and the chauffeur, the four of them could easily get the girl.

Once the chauffeur located the fourth gate, the rickshaw stand was quickly located. The area was bustling with boisterous, jovial coolies eagerly awaiting the night crowd of passengers when they invade Chinatown seeking the fine restaurants and pleasurable clubs available after dark.

Yen Tso walked to the middle of the group hoping to see his nephew Chang as the coolies quickly surrounded him calling out their discounted fares. He was a little uncomfortable with the crowd and called, "Chang, where are you?"

The group of coolies separated making a small path while Wang worked his way through the crowd and stood within inches in front of Yen Tso.

"You mean the elusive Chang? Who wants to know?" Wang said sarcastically.

"I do!" Yen Tso responded with great authority while standing as tall as he could. "You don't know who I am, do you?"

"No," Wang answered with a smart attitude. "Chang is sometimes here and sometimes there. He even may be in Hong Kong. No one knows where he hangs out."

"I'm General Yen Tso… Chang's uncle."

With humility in his voice, while putting a little more space between them, Wang thought: *I should have known him by the white hat. I don't want to make him angry.* Wang respectfully said, "I was expecting Sun Lo to come some time soon to fetch the girl. Where is he? I thought you were in Panama?"

"Don't worry about Sun Lo. He's out of the picture. I'm handling things, now. If Chang isn't here, we will handle this operation by ourselves. We are going to transfer the girl to another location tonight after the quarantined *Ladybug* has sailed out to sea… so we won't have any interference from anyone. I understand there is only one guard on duty inside the warehouse." Yen Tso thought: *Sun Lo must have been confident in his thinking that only one guard was needed to secure the warehouse.*

"Give me a few minutes and I'll look around to see if I can find Chang," Wang offered.

Wang knew he would not find Chang unless he wanted to be found. All the coolies and shopkeepers liked Chang and would never volunteer any information that would bring him harm. Wang made a large circle around the area talking to everyone and looking everywhere to impress Yen Tso and returned: "I guess he's not here, tonight," Wang said nonchalantly.

"Well, then, there will be three of us to get the girl. The *Ladybug* has to move from the harbor by midnight. We will give the ship enough time to clear the harbor area and then we will go to the warehouse," Yen Tso explained as the two men walked toward the limousine.

*****

It was a dark evening, but the bright lights from the entrance at the fourth gate afforded enough light for the surrounding area. Chang witnessed the whole event at the rickshaw stand from a short distance away. He had finished eating at one of the nearby restaurants and was returning to his rickshaw when he noticed the crowd of coolies gathered around someone who was wearing a big white hat. *My uncle so dumb. Everyone know who he is with that big white hat on head. Lucky for me, though.*

Chang was greatly concerned to see his uncle talking to Wang, and he wondered if they were going to go to the warehouse. If so, this was bad timing.

Quan Lee had contacted Chang earlier in the day with the information that General Von was leaving the ship tonight and the plan was to rescue Rachel after midnight. Chang was to meet Seth and Quan Lee at a designated location near the wharf and they would go to the warehouse together, along with General Von. The guard already knew Chang and trusted him to be one of Sun Lo's men, so there should be no problem getting into the warehouse to rescue Rachel.

CHAPTER THIRTY-FOUR

Thick clouds covered the moon carpeting Yokohama in a blanket of darkness. The wharf area was completely void of any sailors, as if no one wanted to venture too close to the *Ladybug*. The quarantine sign served its purpose.

General Von asked Captain Oscarson to keep a vigilant watch over Adam, while the ship waited outside the harbor area… especially with regard to the radio room. He did not want any messages transmitted to Sun Lo.

It was nine o'clock when Captain Oscarson called all his men to the ship's galley for a meeting. Even the deck-watch sailor was asked to leave his post so that no one would be on deck when General Von slipped off the ship. The meeting was purposely long as Captain Oscarson gave a thorough report on communicable diseases and the need for a global surveillance to control the spread of all viruses. He was in his element as a teacher and enjoyed discussing any topic of interest to anyone who would listen. Adam was noticeably restless during the meeting and questioned why General Von was not present. Everyone started to squirm, looking around the room for the general. Captain Oscarson told the men the general was not feeling very well and that he wanted to remain in his room.

This bit of information ignited the slow burning ember of fear in each man. *Could it be possible the disease had already started to spread?*

*****

General Von quietly left the ship unnoticed and found a secluded place to hide on the wharf while he waited for Quan Lee's car to arrive. The black shirt and black hood that he wore provided good camouflage in the darkness. His clothing was nothing compared to the tailored uniform he wore as a German general during World War II, but this rescue mission was the most important confrontation of his whole career. His daughter's life was at stake.

Lights from the dock shimmered on the ripples of the water as the *Ladybug* slowly maneuvered from the dock and sailed toward the open sea. He stared at the ship for a long time… remembering when the ship was involved in another kidnapping attempt to get Rachel. His adversary at that time was also Yen Tso… and he defeated him. In the quiet of the darkness, General Von made a silent promise that he would fight to the death to rescue her.

After the ship sailed into the blackness of night, he turned his attention to the warehouses, which were a short distance farther down the wharf from where he waited. In a squint-eyed manner he focused for clearer vision and noticed a small flickering flame, which sparkled from one of the windows. He was thrilled when he realized, as "doctor" Quan Lee had told him, that the candle in the window was from Rachel's cell. The flame, which was proof that Rachel is still alive, acted as his badge of courage and hope… nourishing his body with renewed vitality.

The chill air from the ocean breeze was penetrating as General Von hunkered down to keep warm… and wait.

*****

The sound of an automobile approaching the wharf area broke the silence arousing General Von's senses, as he did not expect Quan

Lee and the others so soon. His heart pounded at a faster rate and his mind was alert to any surprise that may be a problem. The swinging pole lights cast eerie shadows across the wharf, making it difficult to see the car at a distance. The motor sounded more powerful than the old car Quan Lee had parked at the dock earlier in the day, and General Von decided to sit quietly in the darkness. He remained hidden until he was certain he could identify the car.

I don't believe it... a long black limousine is stopping in front of the warehouse? General Von questioned. He thought perhaps the eye holes cut in his black hood blocked some of his vision and he pulled the hood off his head. He watched as three men got out of the limousine and went into the warehouse where Rachel is held captive. He rubbed his eyes and strained to look again and repeated: *a black limousine. That has to be either Sun Lo or General Yen Tso. What is happening, here! Where is Quan Lee?*

The words were no sooner thought when General Von heard another car. He quickly put on the black hood and waited to see if the car would stop at the designated location at the end of the line of warehouses. It did. Car lights flickered twice, which was Quan Lee's signal. General Von immediately ran to the car, dashing from shadow to shadow and pulled open the car door. There were three men in the car all wearing black shirts and hoods and he breathlessly questioned, "What's going on? Do you see that black limousine parked in front of Rachel's warehouse?"

"Yes," Quan Lee answered and blurted, "That is why we are early. We had to change plans. Get in the car," Quan Lee ordered.

Quan Lee quickly apprised General Von of the latest developments, which included the death of Sun Lo and the visit by Yen Tso to the rickshaw stand. General Von learned that Chang immediately contacted Quan Lee with the news that Yen Tso was going to get the girl right away, which necessitated that their plans had to be changed. Quan Lee and Chang picked up Seth in Chinatown and raced the old car as fast as it would go to meet General Von. They had hoped to arrive at the warehouse before Yen Tso.

General Von listened with interest and surmised, "Well, I guess one of the men in the limousine is Yen Tso. At last, I will meet him face to face."

Chang nervously said, "My Uncle Yen Tso is one very bad man; my no-good friend Wang is other bad man; and limo driver I don't know is other bad man. I glad I have hood on head. I no want uncle to see me."

General Von was quick to add, "We don't know what to expect once we get in the warehouse. I assume they will have Rachel in their custody by the time we arrive. It will be four of us against three of them, plus the guard. We will have to react to the situation once we are inside the warehouse."

Seth sat quietly in the back seat of the car completely oblivious to the conversation. For the past few months, he had lived as an outpost observer for heavy machine guns in Korea, facing death on a day-to-day basis, which had become his way of existence, and he gave no thought for his own safety on this rescue mission. He was totally absorbed with successfully freeing Rachel from her captors… at whatever cost to his own life.

He remembered the many altercations in Hong Kong and the fierce battle in Macau… and his mind rambled with deep concern for the impending struggle to free Rachel. It was one more in a series of life-threatening confrontations, which they had experienced together in the short span of time they have known one another… and they survived them all… and their love grew stronger. He looked upward to the dark heavens above and issued a short prayer that they will share a long life together, sharing a million tomorrows filled with blissful happiness.

All four men removed the black hoods from their head so they could talk more freely. General Von gave a warm smile to Seth and Chang and a few pleasantries were exchanged as Quan Lee maneuvered the old car closer to Rachel's warehouse. The mood was too serious to become involved in chitchat… there would be time for that later.

CHAPTER THIRTY-FIVE

Yen Tso, Wang and the limo driver boldly walked down the long hallway to the guard's station. The guard drew his pistol, but holstered it immediately when he recognized Wang. He assumed the man in the white hat was his boss, Sun Lo, and with no further concern, he picked up the cell keys to open Rachel's door.

This is too easy, Yen Tso thought. But as the guard stumbled down the hallway moaning in pain, Yen Tso surmised: *something is very wrong with this man. There is no way he could put up a fight. And to think Sun Lo thought he had the girl safely guarded. He was a bigger fool than I thought.*

Rachel heard the footsteps in the hallway and immediately braced herself for a confrontation. She did not understand why she would be disturbed so late at night. She could hear by the sound of the boots on the stone floor that there were more men than just the guard coming to her cell. She felt for her sheathed knife under her tunic to make certain it was in place. She tried to stay calm and remembered what Chang had said: "Your father come… soon."

The door opened and from the soft glow from the one candle in the window, Rachel saw three men with the guard. She shook her head in disbelief when she noticed a man wearing a white hat. If her situation were not so serious, she thought it would be funny. *It is strange how your mind plays tricks with your thoughts in adverse conditions.*

Yen Tso made an attempt in English, "You come!"

The guard sat down on the cell floor, holding his groin and moaning in pain. He glared at Rachel as they all left the cell. Yen Tso looked back at the guard as he went out the door and thought: *You pathetic fool! It's a good thing you did not put up a fight, though, or you would be dead now instead of just feeling pain. Um…maybe you are smarter than I thought.*

Yen Tso slowly led the others down the hallway with a stride of confidence, strutting like a peacock thinking he had out-witted General von Horstmann.

Rachel resisted Wang's tug on her arm while he pulled her half dragging and half walking down the long hallway. She did not want to leave the warehouse for fear her father would not be able to find her if she were taken somewhere else. She screamed and kicked, which made Wang laugh louder as he yanked harder on her arm. Yen Tso was already agitated with Rachel and yelled for her to be quiet if she wanted to see the morning sunrise.

The noise of the struggle between Rachel and Wang resounded off the walls of the narrow hall making it impossible for them to hear the door to the warehouse open.

Seth heard Rachel's screams and started to race down the hall. General Von quickly grabbed his arm to hold him back and quietly beckoned for everyone to take a position closer to the walls around the guard's desk in the larger area of the hall. He whispered, "We will stand a better chance of getting Rachel and fighting here than in the narrow hallway.

"Seth, you grab Rachel first and then handle the guard. Quan Lee, you take the chauffeur; and I will handle Yen Tso. Chang, that leaves you with Wang."

With a big smile on his face, Chang turned to Seth and whispered, "Not to worry with guard. He too crippled to fight."

Their black clothing and hoods concealed them from early detection in the dimly lit hall as they pressed against the wall… waiting.

Rachel's screams continued to echo in the halls as she yelled, "Not again!"

Everyone stood frozen... afraid to move as the stone floor beneath their feet suddenly rocked in an up/down motion while small white particles fell from the ceiling. Yen Tso grabbed Rachel's hand from Wang and raced toward the end of the hall with the others in fast pursuit. With a loud snapping sound, a large crack in the floor zigzagged its way down the hall, as the group tried to jostle their steps on the rocking stones. Yen Tso's vision was fixated on the exit at the end of the hall; and as they all ran by the guard's desk, no one paid any attention to the four black objects standing against the wall.

Seth was the first one to jump from the wall to grab Rachel. Another shrilling scream echoed through the halls as Rachel fought the man wearing the black hood. With the fast step of a young African gazelle, General Von pounced on Yen Tso. The men in black used their power of surprise to immobilize Yen Tso and his men of their ability to react quickly. Yen Tso's concentration of sight and thought was to get out of the warehouse before the walls crumbled. He did not expect anyone to be lurking in the shadows of the hall. Everyone paired off as a fierce fight ensued.

Seth gently pushed Rachel aside while he easily fought off the chauffeur with a few martial arts movements that knocked him unconscious. He turned to Rachel to see her pull a knife from under her tunic preparing to fight. Seth quickly yanked the hood from his head; and with a scream of pleasure, Rachel fell into his waiting arms. Her knees became weak as she melted beneath his strong, protective embrace.

The two lovers stole a precious moment from their dangerous situation to hug one another ever so tightly as their emotions escalated to a feverish pitch. The kiss was brief, but the length of time was of no consequence. It was the exchange of passion in their warm, moist lips that would be remembered for a lifetime.

Quan Lee was equally adept in martial arts and quickly subdued Wang while Chang tied him with a heavy cord. No one could see Chang's big grin under his hood when he roughly tied Wang to the desk chair.

Chang ran down the hallway to the cell to check on the Japanese guard. The guard was still sitting on the floor feeling too much pain to move. Chang called to him in Pidgin English, which the guard did not understand, "Earth move. You better move, too."

Quan Lee, Seth and Rachel stood watching General Von and Yen Tso fight. It was a savage fight with no weapons used... just fists, strength and skill... they wanted to kill with their bare hands. The fighting lasted for many minutes as the men were evenly matched. At one point, General Von was knocked against the wall and stood dazed for a moment. Quan Lee used this break to take General Von's place in the bitter fight with Yen Tso.

Quan Lee removed his hood and for a moment stood before his childhood friend... ready to avenge Yen Tso's shame and misery he had brought upon his family and the people of the fishing village of Aberdeen. Yen Tso's look of surprise was worth the long wait. Quan Lee braced himself for the encounter to exact satisfaction.

General Von shook off his dizziness and motioned to Quan Lee that he wanted to get back into the fight. Quan Lee shook his head, no, and forcibly said, "Yen Tso is mine."

Many childhood memories went through their minds as the men remembered all the times they had played and fought as children. They grew up like brothers, knowing each other's every move and thoughts. Every blow was meant to be death-dealing and the vicious fighting continued while the others helplessly stood and watched.

The warehouse slowly started to crumble, as the walls moved and the floor vibrated from more earth temblors.

Quan Lee held Yen Tso tightly against the wall, staring into his eyes, and was poised to kill him with his knife. After a moment and in the blink-of-an-eye, Yen Tso managed to grab Quan Lee by the throat with his left hand and with his right hand, he swiftly plunged his knife deep into Quan Lee.

Yen Tso snarled, "Why did you hesitate? Did you have a weak moment of compassion for an old friend? You were always a fool... even as kids I could beat you at every game we played.

Quan Lee fell to the floor amidst what sounded like the drumbeat of a driving rain.

Debris from the crumbling walls covered the floor as General Von made his way across the area to attack Yen Tso, who with a mean smile on his face beckoned him. General Von ripped his hood

Candle in the Window

from his head and demanded, "Seth, you and Chang take Rachel outside where it is safe."

Rachel screamed with happiness, "Father, father!"

General Von yelled, again, "Get Rachel out of here, now!"

Only Chang ran toward the door.

"I won't go without you!" Rachel cried.

Small temblors continued, which motion aroused the chauffeur, who was lying unconscious on the floor. He easily surveyed the situation and hopped to his feet with an anxious desire to leave the warehouse. Wang looked at him with appealing eyes and pleaded, "Untie my ropes! Help me!"

The chauffeur grabbed his knife, which was still lying on the floor, and with a quick slice of the ropes, he freed Wang. Both men ran at great speed toward the door. As far as they were concerned, the fight was over. They were running for their life.

Chang excitedly called, "Water! Water! Big water come fast!"

Chang's warning did not phase General Von nor Yen Tso. They were oblivious to any sound that would detract them, while their eyes stayed focused in a burning hatred.

Seth held tightly to Rachel's hand as the two ran for the door. Rachel looked back several times to see her father and Yen Tso wrestling on the floor, as the walls started to give way to the shaking earth.

It was Yen Tso who broke away from the fierce fight... quickly searched for his white hat and ran for the door, as water started to flow into the hall with tremendous force as if the water were ejected from a fire hose.

Seth and Rachel stood holding one another tightly, yet frozen at the door, standing in water ankle deep waiting for General Von, as Yen Tso ran past them splashing in the water violently in a bewildered state of frenzy trying to escape while holding his white hat tightly in his hand.

The water receded with a loud sucking sound, and within minutes there was a deafening noise as if ten freight trains were converging at one time on the wharf. Seth, Rachel and General Von ran as fast as they could toward higher ground, but the swirling syrupy brown water from the giant wave caught them with unimaginable force.

Seth and Rachel tried to hold fast together, but their strength could not possibly match the force of the water. Swimming was not an option as the water raged in its own powerfully angry style. The three were carried farther inland, tumbling over and over again underwater, thrashing vigorously to surface grasping for breath.

At one time, the water lifted their legs, where they had no control, and held them horizontally. They called and screamed frantically for one another, but the roar of the water drowned any sound for help. A tempest of chaotic, troublesome thoughts rambled around in their minds.

Rachel could not believe that she had been rescued after weeks of captivity only to die in a giant wave of water. Her thoughts quickly reverted to her childhood memories of living in Paris in an orphanage, where an every day struggle for survival revolved around the War. The orphanage on the island of Lantau in China quickly came to mind, where she helped to create a happy environment for homeless children; and she worked with her father... often times in a risky surveillance capacity dealing with the Triad hoodlums' smuggling opium. She thought her heart would burst with fear that she may never see Seth again. She remembered their short, wonderful courtship in Hong Kong, which filled a void in her life with a love so consuming that she could not fathom living without him. She had to live through this catastrophic ordeal... and Seth must live, also. In retrospect, she thought she could have the best of both worlds... living and working in the orphanage, which she loved, and marrying Seth, who would have to live on Lantau with her. She realized for the first time that her heart's desire... her first love... was to be with Seth for the rest of her life and that would involve moving to the plantation in Virginia. She wished she had married Seth when they were in the States, and she realized she never should have returned to Lantau. She cried to herself, *Seth, where are you. I love you so much it hurts. Please, live!*

Seth was frantic with worry for Rachel as random thoughts quickly went through his mind. With his arms tightly wrapped around her, he desperately tried to hold her close to him when the big wave hit. His strength was no match for the powerful water, which suddenly pulled her away. He remembered how beautiful she looked the first time he saw her on a sampan in Victoria Harbor in Hong Kong. He could not believe that he would find his soul mate half way around the world. It was love at first sight and he vowed at that time there never would be anything that would separate them... but the irony of life has a funny way of dealing out circumstances where you have no control. He was drafted into the army. His thoughts lingered for a moment on the terrible battles he fought in Korea. He managed to live through those fire fights; he lived through the fierce battle aboard the *Ladybug* in Macau a year and a half ago, and now he must live through this horrendous battle of surviving the ocean's wave. With a heavy heart he made another vow to Rachel, that if they both lived through this ordeal, and after they married, they never would be separated, again. He cried to himself, *Rachel, where are you? Don't give up. Please, live for me.*

General Von was furious with himself for ever letting Rachel help him with certain, "safe" surveillance operations in dealing with the drug dealers. He thought: *my goodness, what was I thinking! I was sacrificing my daughter's life. There are no "safe" surveillance operations. She never should have returned to Lantau. She should have married Seth and stayed in Virginia. I guess her first love was to help the little children in the orphanage. If we all survive this nightmare, I hope she will want to live in Virginia on the plantation she inherited.*

The three surfaced again and noticed they were about a hundred feet apart at this time. Each one was surprised and happy to see the other as the wave continued to carry them toward a small knoll of earth. Within minutes the area was an inland sea. It looked as if the whole ocean were boiling with a mixture of everything imaginable floating in the churning brown water. Each one grabbed hold of an object that could keep them afloat as the wave, which had suddenly swept them farther inland, now abruptly retreated. The area was littered with debris from the receding water and the three were miraculously dropped on the ground.

Totally exhausted, wet and dirty from the muddy water, they gathered enough strength to trudge up the hill toward one another, grinning with happiness, and not fully comprehending how they all managed to survive. All three embraced, giving thanks to God that they were all saved. Seth and Rachel fell together in a crushing hug, kissed and fell to the ground holding each other. For the first time in many weeks, Rachel felt safe and secure while Seth continued to hold her tightly in his arms. With ambivalent emotions, she wept tears of happiness and tears of sadness, as they sat stunned with disbelief as to what they were witnessing. They watched as the receding water raged in swirling eddies of white foam. Power lines along the wharf sagged to the ground from teetering utility poles. Fishing boats were torn from their moorings and furiously bobbed up and down like fishing corks on rough water.

Seth, Rachel and General Von were horrified to see the water level in the harbor suddenly drop, sucking many ships out to sea, while in the harbor, massive cargo ships converged in a tight circle as the water swirled and the masses of steel collided like bumper cars at a county fair. Albeit the full force of the tsunami did not hit the Yokohama harbor area, the carnage was reminiscent of the atomic bombs that were dropped on Hiroshima and Nagasaki in 1945. These killer waves were caused by a natural disaster creating chaos in a dramatic style showing no mercy. The warehouses along the wharf were ransacked by the waves and the coast was littered with pieces of boats, fish and every earthly thing. The tremendous power of the water threw everything around as easily as tossing a rag doll, creating loud sounds of things crashing as if the whole earth were breaking.

They sat quietly for many minutes… each one thinking about what they had just experienced. They sat paralyzed with disbelief. How did they manage to survive? Each one became mesmerized with prayerful thoughts when the silence was broken.

"That some big wave. I no want to go on ocean anymore," Chang bemoaned. "I kick myself if I get off dry land."

The three stared in disbelief when they saw Chang holding a large white hat in his hand walking toward them from the far side of the small round hill. He sat down beside them and told his story of survival.

"Many times, I go up/down in muddy water. I hold on to this tree and that wood box or something. I think I choke many times from bad water. Finally, wave plop me down on ground like she tired of carrying me. I very happy and sit to watch wave go away." Chang sat for a few minutes and said nothing as if wanting to forget what happened next. "I see Uncle Tso in water. He wave white hat at me and call for help. He look very mean. Like he kill me if I no save him. I tried." With a feeling of guilt, Chang continued, slowly. "I not try too hard. Angry wave carry him out to sea and leave white hat behind in wood crate. I fetch hat, but not uncle. He go fast with wave."

Chang rubbed the hat with both hands and brightly said, "This hat lucky charm for Uncle Tso. Maybe luck rub on me." After more thought, he decided, "Hat not lucky for Uncle. He die. Maybe not lucky for me." Chang threw the hat as far as he could into the murky water as they all watched the hat float out to sea.

CHAPTER THIRTY-SIX

Early morning daylight exposed a nightmare of devastation never before seen by the four who sat on the knoll of a small hill dazed with disbelief. The panoramic view revealed a landscape of destruction caused by the tsunami when it unleashed its power. There were only two great harbor waves, but it was enough to wreak havoc in taking human life and destroying everything in its path.

Rachel, Seth, General Von and Chang sat on the knoll for a long time, as the hours they spent fighting to survive in the water deprived them of their physical strength. They were drained from exhaustion, making it difficult for them to understand fully the depth of their predicament. Their mental disposition lacked the ability to grasp the reality of their surviving this wretched experience and they continued to sit in silence. They noticed many spectators who gathered on the bluffs that surround Yokohama at Harbor View Hill Park started to descend on the devastated area in an effort to find any survivors.

As time passed, more and more people appeared in the area, walking like zombies from another planet, in search for loved ones. They walked aimlessly... in no particular direction... as if lost, hoping to recognize someone. It was evident that the strength of the tsunami was not powerful enough to quell the human spirit, as the survivors stumbled along in good faith resisting an unfathomable hardship.

The sights, smells and sounds began to penetrate the senses of the four who lingered longer than desired; and as if by general consensus, they decided to seek refuge somewhere to reclaim a semblance of livelihood. Chang was quick to offer his friend's home where Seth had found comfort for a few days. It was a long, arduous walk, but they knew there would be food, water and clean clothing at the end of the journey. They all agreed it was a good idea and the four set out for Chinatown. Dirty, weary and hungry, they had walked only a short distance, with energy that was quickly failing, when Chang hailed a few of his coolie friends and asked them for a ride in their rickshaws. The coolies were eager to help the survivors of the great wave and the four sat comfortably in the rickshaws. Chang was the hero of the moment.

*****

The Chinese tailor and his wife were very happy to see Chang, Seth and his friends, as they had heard all about the giant wave that crushed the harbor. They extended the usual politeness wanting to please their guests, knowing from their appearance they had experienced a terrible ordeal. The guests were immediately offered the facilities to bathe, while the wife prepared a warm supper of fish and rice. Nippon Beer and sake were served, also, completing a generous meal, which more than satisfied their appetite. They sat and relaxed in their clean clothes, which the tailor provided, realizing that only a few short hours ago they were floundering in the murky water for survival. They knew they were blessed.

After resting for an hour, General Von asked Chang to take him to the nearest Western Union office so he could send a cable to the American doctor in the army hospital in Tokyo. It was imperative that the doctor cable Captain Oscarson with the news of their survival and the necessity for the *Ladybug* to return to port. He had to alert Captain Oscarson to the circumstances that now prevail.

*****

Candle in the Window

Captain Oscarson was well aware of the strange movement of the water as the *Ladybug* continued to roll on angry waves as the ship sailed farther away from the harbor. In his many years as a merchant seaman, sailing all the seas in the world, he had never experienced a harbor wave. He remembered reading about one of the worst tidal waves ever recorded in history that destroyed the Minoan Greek culture on the island of Crete in the Mediterranean Sea in 1450 B.C., which was struck by a two-hundred-foot tidal wave; he knew that a tsunami, a term for a Japanese harbor wave, typically occurs about every six years in the Pacific Ocean along the Pacific Rim; and he certainly never wanted to experience a tsunami first hand. He wondered if his friends on shore were safe.

It was early morning as he stood on deck looking far across the water toward the harbor. His thoughts were interrupted when the seaman from the radio room delivered a cable to him from the port authorities. It read: "Doctor advises sailor does not have a communicable disease and ship may return to harbor. Suggest you wait two days before entering as many boats were destroyed and rest abandoned. Use great caution. Contact doctor upon arrival. Friends are all OK."

Captain Oscarson had not finished reading the message when the radio man spread the good news to everyone aboard ship that the *Ladybug* was no longer under quarantine. The sullen disposition of the crewmen changed to anxiety to unload the ship's cargo immediately so they could enjoy a short leave on shore. Yokohama's reputation for having lively nightlife establishments was always an incentive for the crewmen to work quickly and they did not relish the idea of having to wait two days longer at sea. They were pleased, however, that they would not have to fear the possibility of a flu epidemic aboard ship, which would make their daily chore of chipping and painting less stressful.

*****

Two days of idle time on the *Ladybug* while it waited at sea to return to the harbor provided an opportunity for Adam to reflect upon his dire situation. He believed General Von did not suspect him of being the traitor in planning Rachel's kidnapping; so for now, he felt safe, but he knew he had to get off the ship in Yokohama. Instead of making plans to escape, he yearned for Rachel's love. He could think of nothing else as his thoughts turned morbid with wanting to punish her for not returning his love. Something had snapped in his mind... and he became a man possessed... tormented with love turning to hate.

When he arrived on the island of Lantau to work for General Von, Adam was a likeable young man in his mid-twenties with a nice smile to match an easy-going disposition. His credentials were exemplary having worked for the British Intelligence office in London; and after only one year of service, General Von made him one of his key lieutenants... treating him almost as a son.

There were a few times when Rachel and Adam worked closely together on certain surveillance operations in Hong Kong where they developed a mutual friendship of trust in performance of their duty. Too quickly, Adam mistook Rachel's friendship for love and he became a zealous admirer, seeking Rachel's affection. She suggested to her father that she should not continue to be a partner with Adam as he made her feel very uneasy when he started to make advances to her, which she neither liked nor appreciated. There was no one who could ever replace Seth for her devotion and love.

Adam continued to fantasize that he could capture Rachel's love even though she never encouraged his advances. His delusion reached its peak when he attempted to break into Rachel's bedroom one night. General Von was awakened and immediately ran to Rachel's room as Adam climbed out the window. Rachel was startled, but nothing happened; and after admonishing Adam, General Von let the intrusion pass as a love-sick young man going out of control. Rachel and General Von put the incident behind them after Adam apologized.

Adam stayed in his cabin most of the time... not wanting to talk to any of the crew about his reason for being aboard the ship. The crewmen had no knowledge of Rachel's kidnapping or the opium being smuggled in the rice barrels so they had no reason to believe anything but that he and General Von were merely passengers traveling from Canton to Yokohama. He was very uncomfortable...

feeling cloistered on the ship with no way to escape if General Von should find out he was the one who betrayed Rachel. He knew he had no control over his present condition of being confined to the ship, and he still felt no remorse in being a double agent and taking the money in return for the information he sold to Sun Lo and Yen Tso regarding the time and place for the kidnapping. With distorted thoughts, his warped mind compelled him to hurt Rachel, which would compensate for his love-sick misery. He became worried when he had not seen General Von for quite awhile, and he wondered if his absence during mealtimes was due to sickness. All these thoughts were running through his mind when he heard a knock on his cabin door.

"Adam," Captain Oscarson called. "Are you all right?"

Adam opened the door with apprehension. "Yes. Why?"

The two men stood looking at one another for a few seconds when the captain responded, "You didn't look very well this morning at breakfast and I thought perhaps you were still seasick."

"I'm fine, but I'm concerned for General Von. I haven't seen him for awhile. Is he still not feeling well?"

"Oh, that," Captain Oscarson nonchalantly volunteered, "he left the ship the other night to rescue Rachel and the cable I received this morning said that everyone is okay. I guess that tells us that Rachel is safe. What great news!"

Captain Oscarson turned to leave the cabin hiding a smile on his face as he noticed Adam turned white upon hearing the news. He wanted to plant the seed of fear in him for the anguish he had caused Rachel and General Von. As far as he was concerned, throwing him overboard to the sharks would be a just punishment.

Adam closed the door and fell back onto his cot, shaking with fear, as the palms of his hands became sweaty when he rubbed them together. He really needed a cigarette.

CHAPTER THIRTY-SEVEN

The two days that Rachel and Seth spent together in Chinatown were days filled with happiness in planning their future. They spent many quiet hours in the comfort of the tailor's home enjoying the opportunity to be together. After all they had been through in the past several weeks, it was difficult for them to comprehend how their lives intertwined once again. They believed it was destiny that continued to bring them together even through adverse times… and their love grew evermore stronger.

"Do you want to tell me what happened in the warehouse during those terrible days when you were held captive?" Seth asked.

"No. Not now. Maybe some day I will be able to look back on it and not cry. For now, I want to put those horrible weeks out of my mind," she quietly lamented lowering her head and in a humbled murmur she continued. "When you have a desperate need, a reverent feeling for anything that will bring you hope, becomes your salvation. Placing the candle in the window was my symbol of hope… hope to be rescued… hope that I would see you again and hope that you would love me always." She softly cried as Seth tried to comfort her.

They decided that Rachel would return to the States to live on her plantation in Virginia and wait for Seth to return from his tour of duty in Korea. They wanted a big wedding with all the trimmings, and, of course, they wanted to be married immediately. They bubbled over with happiness and enthusiasm planning their wedding, not fully being able to understand how life could be so good. Seth put his thoughts of having to return to the war in Korea out of his mind. He did not want to spoil their short, marvelous time with depressive thoughts. He prayed they would continue to be blessed.

"Ya know what, Rachel?" Seth questioned.

"No. What?" Rachel coyly asked.

"I love you." And Seth held her ever so closely and kissed her tenderly.

These words were spoken quite often during the course of the day with the ritual becoming a little game they played. Often times, Rachel would respond with, "Yes, I know you love me."

Their love was a deep fulfilling experience... a positive, passionate emotion that they planned to cultivate into powerful loving spirits... they were soul mates.

*****

General Von was busy during the two days waiting for the *Ladybug* to return to the harbor. His first order of business was to go to the narcotics division in Tokyo where preparations were made to confiscate the barrels of opium from the ship's cargo hold, bringing that operation to a successful conclusion.

Of urgent importance, was to contact the Pentagon in Washington, D.C. to advise that Seth's furlough to Japan in helping with his daughter's rescue mission was now complete and that Seth could return to Korea to finish his tour of duty. The general was most gracious in his thanks to the Pentagon for the army allowing Seth to participate in a successful coup. He introspectively gave thanks for having friends in "high places".

Lastly, but of equal importance, was to have Sydney's body returned to her family in England. The general deeply regretted the loss of a fine comrade and wrote a glowing letter of her ability and loyalty, which he mailed immediately. He also felt remorse for losing another valued friend... Quan Lee. He immediately wrote a letter to Quan Lee's relatives explaining how he died a brave death fighting Yen Tso; and the general wrote of his regret in not being able to fulfill Quan Lee's wishes to be buried in the Permanent Cemetery in Aberdeen. With deep condolences, the general wrote that Quan Lee and Yen Tso were both washed out to sea in the tsunami.

General Von had many regrets about this operation, but the thrill of having his daughter safely in his care helped to compensate for losing two fine people… Sydney and Quan Lee.

CHAPTER THIRTY-EIGHT

An old taxi weaved a narrow path through debris, which remained along the whole general area of the wharf. The great wave left its mark leaving acres of devastation that remained to be cleared. The port authorities were anxious to clear the harbor of the derelict boats first, so supplies from merchant ships could be brought into Yokohama. It was evident that restoration of the area would take much longer than two days. Thankfully, the area was washed in moonlight as there was no electricity on the boardwalk to light the way as the taxi driver carefully drove closer to the water's edge where the dock had been.

It was not a joyous ride from the tailor's home to the harbor as Rachel, Seth and General Von sat quietly immersed in a single thought: *Tomorrow, Seth is returning to Korea.*

The *Ladybug* was anchored in the harbor a short distance from the dock area, as there was too much destruction for the ship to pull closer. Captain Oscarson provided a lifeboat from the *Ladybug* to bring them aboard. All three brightened when they saw Captain Oscarson standing at the ship's railing to welcome them.

"You are a welcomed sight to behold!" Captain Oscarson called as the small lifeboat tied to the ship.

The three climbed the rope ladder to board the ship... each with a big smile, happy to see their old friend. Seth was the first one to give Captain Oscarson a handshake, which quickly turned into a strong hug as the two embraced. Seth never thought he would ever see the captain again… a man who became his mentor and surrogate father during his voyage from Le Havre to Hong Kong.

Captain Oscarson escorted the three to the dining hall where they could talk more comfortably while enjoying a light supper. The hour quickly melted away as the three told the story of Rachel's rescue and their horrendous experience of surviving the tsunami. The captain sat spellbound… not asking any questions, as he believed he was a witness to a miracle that all three lived to tell their story.

The crewmen had all returned to the ship from a night's leave in Yokohama and were quite festive in their mood, which raucous activity alerted the captain that they enjoyed the evening on shore and, most importantly, that it was time for the ship to sail for Hong Kong.

The captain grabbed Seth by the shoulders in a fatherly gesture and suggested, "Let's hope the next time we meet it will be under happier circumstances."

Seth wholeheartedly agreed.

Seth and Rachel were the first to leave the dining hall together, as they wanted to have a few minutes to themselves on deck before Seth had to return to Chinatown. Rachel tried to be strong, holding back tears and mournfully lamented, "All I have done these past few weeks is cry. Oh, Seth, I want to be happy." She looked with tear-filled eyes into his eyes and continued, "And that means I want to be with you."

Seth softly answered, holding her ever so closely, "Don't cry Rachel." His eyes betrayed his bravery, saying, "The more sadness in parting… the more joy in the reunion."

Good-byes are never long enough when two people never want to leave each other. They lingered for several minutes longer, not saying anything… just holding one another. Finally, after a passionate kiss good-bye, Seth started to walk toward the rope ladder to leave the ship when he turned, "Ya know what, Rachel?" he asked.

She wanted to play their little game to hear him say it one more time… and coyly asked, "No, what?"

"I love you."

*****

Candle in the Window

Captain Oscarson's decision to sail to Hong Kong, instead of his next destination, which was Panama, was decided to accommodate General Von's wishes that Adam be turned over to the narcotics authorities in China. General Von wanted them to determine Adam's punishment. He knew he would be too harsh in judgment... as he felt he could strangle him with his bare hands for the tremendous anguish and living hell he caused his daughter.

Captain Oscarson mentioned to the general, "I had a short conversation with Adam, and he showed extreme nervousness when I told him you and Rachel were alive. As far as I can tell, he does not realize that you are aware that he is the traitor."

"That's good. Let's keep it that way. His surprise will come when we get to Hong Kong. But let's keep a close eye on him during our voyage."

The ship started to rock as it sailed into deeper water. Rachel continued to stand at the railing looking toward the harbor, hoping for one more chance to see Seth.

CHAPTER THIRTY-NINE

The morning was gloomy with the sky overcast in gray clouds when Seth awoke. Even bright sunlight could not have lifted his spirits as he prepared to leave Chinatown for his flight to Korea. It was a sleepless night as his vision of seeing Rachel standing on deck of the *Ladybug* the evening before kept replaying in his dreams and it was almost more than he could handle. Once again, they had to be separated.

Chang came to the tailor's home earlier than expected to give Seth a ride in his rickshaw to the taxi stand as he wanted to spend more time with him. Once again, they had survived a harrowing experience which brought them even closer into a brotherly friendship. Chang took a slow, circuitous route to the taxi stand as he did not want to see Seth leave. They talked and laughed about anything that would keep their thoughts away from Seth's impending flight to Korea.

"Chang, are you going to stay in Japan?" Seth questioned. "I thought you would want to sail with General Von and Rachel to Hong Kong."

"No, not me." Chang was quick to answer. "Mean dream at night play bad game with me. I under angry brown wave drowning and I wake up wet all over in pool of water. Body shake and teeth bounce. I try to close eyes to sleep, but I still see water swirl 'round me." Chang shuddered to repeat it. "I no like take bath no more. Water too high in tub. I in bad way." Chang sighed and continued, "I have number one idea: I stay in Chinatown with friends."

"Well, you can always fly to Hong Kong," Seth suggested.

"That no good, too. I no like to fly." With a brilliant thought, he exclaimed, "Maybe ask feng shui master how to get to Hong Kong."

Seth smiled at his friend with a look of assurance that perhaps that would be a good idea.

A gentle rain started to fall as the rickshaw pulled into the taxi stand. Both men stood quietly beside the rickshaw with a myriad of emotions racing through their heads, wondering what would be the odds of ever seeing one another again. They had been together twice under extremely hazardous circumstances, creating a bond of fraternal trust. Could it be possible that they would meet for a third time?

Chang broke the silence and stammered, "If feng shui agree, I like our paths to cross again some day."

With one last embrace Seth said, "I would like that."

CHAPTER FORTY

Seth was late to arrive at the airport for his flight to Korea as the early morning shower dampened the road to a slippery surface, causing the taxi driver to use more caution and less speed. A long line of military personnel had already formed on the tarmac waiting to board a Globe Master cargo plane to take them to Korea. Seth looked at the plane in amazement, wondering how a plane that big could ever get off the ground. The sergeant started counting the number of men in line who would board the plane; stopped counting at the man right in front of Seth and urged the men to board the Globe Master. Seth and the rest of the men behind him would have to wait for another plane. The rain became a driving force pelting the tarmac while the remaining men ran to a Quonset hut, which was a short distance away to take refuge. The mood of the men was fraught with somber thoughts as they knew they were returning to a hostile environment where a fatalistic attitude toward death was an every-day practice… where if you get killed, you get killed. They lived with death, wondering which one of their buddies would be next.

It was extremely difficult for Seth to get back into that frame of mind, especially after being with Rachel for a few days. He sat silently, as all the men did, wondering where in Korea he would find the 145th automatic weapons battalion. He remembered Major Tamermia told him they were moving up north to the Iron Triangle area. He had much to think about on his flight to Kimpo Airbase outside Seoul, South Korea.

*****

It was late afternoon when the plane landed at Kimpo Airbase and the men were immediately loaded on trucks to take them to their destination. At nighttime, the truck stopped at a Quonset hut along the way where Seth and the others slept on the floor. The next day, they were driven to the Chorwon Valley within six miles from the main line of resistance, where he was reinstated with his outfit.

The truck rolled into camp dodging the soldiers who were walking to the mess tent. It was suppertime and Seth was eager to get some chow as he had not eaten since breakfast, but first he wanted to put his duffel bag in his tent. He heard a loud voice call, "Seth! Over here." It was Ian who was emerging from his tent and beckoned Seth.

With a surprised look on his face and a big grin, Ian happily asked, "Hey, man, what are you doing here? We thought you were killed on the Globe Master that crashed into the mountainside near Seoul during the rainstorm."

A little dazed with disbelief, Seth asked, "What?"

"Yeah, we heard you were scheduled to fly on that plane. I'm sure glad they were wrong."

Not quite able to comprehend what he had just heard, Seth said, "Yeah! Me, too!"

Ian jokingly asked, "Did you miss us?"

Seth gave a side-glance look at Ian with a silly smirk and said nothing.

Seth slowly entered the tent… taking his time looking around at a place he would call home for the next few months. After the harrowing experiences of the last few days, and now learning that he could have been killed had he boarded the Globe Master… and he was only one man away from that happening… he was not emotionally ready to face these conditions and the possibility of more fire fights. He knew he would have to fortify himself with strong convictions

Candle in the Window

to survive this war, believing his life is all worthwhile because of Rachel.

Ian had no problem in reading the expression on Seth's face. He had just returned from his R-and-R in Japan and he knew how difficult it was to return to Korea.

Ian urged, "Come on, Seth, let's go get some chow. I know you missed the food, here."

Seth looked at Ian and said, "Yeah, right." Both men laughed as they trudged through the snow to the mess tent.

*****

Once again, Major Tamermia was in charge of the courts-martial cases and called Seth to the command tent for assistance in typing the papers. Seth entered the tent, saluted the major and was asked to sit down beside the major's desk.

"Welcome back, corporal. It's good to see you again." And with more deliberation, the major added, "I guess you could write a book about your experiences in Japan. I have a few minutes. Why don't you tell me about the tsunami?"

The two soldiers sat for a long time as Seth shared his story with the major. Seth began with General Von's request for him to assist in Rachel's rescue; the terrible experience of living through the great wave of the tsunami and ending with his narrow escape from being killed on the Globe Master. In retrospect, Seth added with astonishment, "I don't know how I lived through it all."

"Corporal, you have the 'luck of Custer'." Major Tamermia was quick to add.

Seth asked, "I don't understand? He was killed at the Little Big Horn."

"Oh, yes, that's right. His luck did not sustain him through that battle." The major proudly continued, "Do you remember when I told you about the military history of my family? My great grandfather served under Custer at the battle of the Little Big Horn and he believed he, along with the regiment, would always have the 'luck of Custer'. Those words became a slogan and it was mentioned many times among soldiers who knew the story about General Custer leading seven cavalry charges in one campaign during the Civil War... and he survived unscathed." The major shook his head up and down and quietly repeated, "The 'luck of Custer' that is what every soldier wants. I believe we had a little bit of that luck with us a week ago when we were in the Iron Triangle."

With a forceful voice, the major commanded, "I don't want you volunteering for night patrols or doing anything silly that will put your life in jeopardy. You'll be going home in a few months."

Seth took those words as good advice. The word "home" conjured up the plans that he and Rachel had made, which included a big wedding on the plantation. With a peaceful, happy thought, he quietly said, "Let's hope I have the 'luck of Custer'."

CHAPTER FORTY-ONE

The ship's cabin was small and poorly furnished; but to Rachel, it was a luxurious room compared to her cell in the old warehouse. The gentle roll of the waves rocked her bed with the motion of a cradle helping to relax her body from the stress of the previous days. Her mind, however, kept hopping from one thought to another as the ship's bell tolled the hour many times before she decided to concentrate only on the future of her life with Seth and to put other concerns out of her mind. After trying to get into a sleep-inducing position, she punched the pillow several times, thought about her wedding plans, and with a smile on her lips she finally drifted off to sleep.

The staccato beat of rain on the porthole awakened her at an early hour. A new day was starting with bad weather, but to Rachel, it was the beginning of a great day... she was sailing home with her father. Everything that morning was great... the shower before breakfast; clean clothes, which the tailor provided; sitting at the table talking with her father; and breathing the fresh sea air. Never again would she take the simple things in life for granted.

General Von anticipated that Rachel would want to talk to him about certain things and he surmised most of the discussion would involve Seth. It was easy to see the two were in love.

It had been some time since he and Rachel had sat down to discuss anything of a serious nature regarding her future. The two reminisced about the chat they had over two years ago regarding her traveling to Virginia to verify the validity of her birth to satisfy the courts that she was the heiress to inherit a large tobacco plantation. At that time, General Von wanted her to live on the plantation as he feared she would want to become more involved in his dangerous profession if she stayed in China. Her involvement seemed to mushroom over the years and now he was going to put an end to it.

"I want you to promise me one thing, Rachel," General Von stated. "I want you to promise that you will never again get involved in my work. You're a beautiful, young lady and you should start thinking of building a future for yourself. Maybe, you should take a more administrative position in the orphanage on Lantau. All the children love you and I know they are really worried about you." He knew this was a selfish thought as he did not want her to leave home, but he was driven by fatherly love to suggest it. More slowly, he continued, "Or perhaps, you should return to Virginia and make a new life for yourself on the plantation."

General Von knew that she had given her heart to Seth as it was easy to read her emotions when the two were together. He looked at Rachel and noticed the gleam in her eyes when he mentioned that she return to Virginia. Knowing what the answer would be, he lowered his head and stammered, "Although if you go to Virginia, I will really miss you."

A full minute passed before Rachel slowly said, "Dad, I'm glad you brought that up. There is something I want to tell you." Rachel took a deep breath, "Seth and I are going to be married as soon as he is mustered out of the army."

General Von expected to hear this, but it still hurt as he knew she would be leaving for a lifetime. He coughed a little, choking with fatherly emotions, and managed to say brightly, "Congratulations! But I'm not surprised. I can tell you are both very much in love. I think Seth is a great young man and you have my blessings."

CHAPTER FORTY-TWO

Vibrant colors from sunrays streaked across the heavens parting the rain clouds into beautiful patches of clear blue sky. A glorious rainbow appeared off the bow of the ship, which Rachel believed was a sign of good luck.

Good sailing weather was with them all the way from Japan to Hong Kong. Fortunately, the trip was peaceful and uneventful, which Rachel and General Von much appreciated as they had lived through a nightmare of experiences that would last them a lifetime. Rachel spent most of the day on deck in the brilliant sunshine daydreaming while sitting on top of a high storage chest at the bow of the ship. She used this time to contemplate her wedding and her new life living on the plantation. It was easy for her to drift into a peaceful meditative mode with the slow rock of the ship on the calm sea and the gentle breeze blowing her long blonde hair.

General Von interrupted her thoughts when he called her attention to an albatross circling high in the bright blue sky. "What a beautiful, majestic bird. All seafaring wanderers believe this bird is an omen of good fortune. It soars with a feeling of freedom and confidence."

"Oh, father, I want to feel as free and confident as the albatross. Do you think some day I will be able to forget being kidnapped and living in that dreadful cell?"

"I'm certain of it." General Von asserted. "You have your whole future before you. That's beautiful in itself. You and Seth have a strong foundation of love on which to build a treasure trove of experiences together and you will see… your thoughts will dwell on the beautiful things in life, and time will erase the ugly remembrances from your mind."

The two sat side-by-side discussing everything important to a young woman. This was a rare opportunity for Rachel to be able to have her father's attention for so long a time. His professional duties and diligence in handling the responsibilities of his office always deprived them of time being spent together. She thought, *this is a great day!*

General Von's thoughts were bitter-sweet. He was thrilled with rescuing his daughter from her kidnappers; and if it had not been for the tsunami, the operation would have gone fairly smoothly. Occasionally, he would think about Sydney and Quan Lee and how valuable they were in contributing to the success of freeing Rachel. He would always hold them in his fond memories.

He was also very pleased he was able to confiscate the whole shipment of opium and turn it over to the narcotics division in Tokyo. And working with his old friend, Captain Oscarson, was a blessing he never could have imagined.

His thoughts turned to Yen Tso and Sun Lo… two of the most diabolic examples of men steeped in wickedness. He thought, *the world will be a better place without them, but I regret there always will be someone to take their place.* In his command of the post on the island of Lantau, he will continue to fight against gold smugglers and drug traffickers in the Orient to rid the area of the scum who feast like vultures on their own kind. In his strength of confidence, he will continue to strive for an environment where the evil element will be harnessed. He believed his work justified his decision and thought, *I have made my home on the island of Lantau and I will have to be content with visiting Rachel in Virginia on special occasions. I also have the orphanage to consider. All those little children count on me for a safe home… and I will not disappoint them.*

"Isn't this a spectacular day!" Caption Oscarson called to the two sitting on the storage chest. "May I sit with you for a few minutes?"

"Of course!" General Von assured, welcoming him. How's my good friend, Adam, feeling today?" he asked facetiously with a wink of the eye.

Rachel broke into the conversation, "Yes, where has he been this whole trip? He doesn't take meals in the dining room and he never comes on deck"

General Von inserted, "I haven't seen him since the *Ladybug* left Yokohama and I don't want to see him until we dock in Hong Kong. I have nothing to say to him. He's the traitor and he's been caught."

"He's a traitor? What do you mean?" Rachel questioned.

"The strategy of the time and place for your abduction was all planned by Adam. Do you remember being forced into the large dragon float at the Chinese festival parade in Hong Kong and being taken to Yokohama?"

"Yes. I was hit on the head pretty hard so I can't recall everything. I remember waking up in that terrible, smelly cell and not knowing where I was... and what was most frightening, I couldn't remember my name."

General Von became livid when he heard all the details of his daughter's abduction and continued: "There were several little things he did where his actions became questionable and it became obvious that he was a traitor. At that point, I made certain that he was with me at all times so I could keep a close watch on him. I took him with me to Canton where we boarded the *Ladybug*, which miraculously had been commissioned to carry the opium to Yokohama. I decided at that time he would never leave the ship until I could turn him over to the proper authorities in Hong Kong."

Rachel interrupted to exclaim, "I knew Adam hated me for rejecting his love, but I never thought he would go so far as to have me kidnapped."

General Von continued, "When the ship was allowed to enter the harbor after the tsunami damage was partially cleared, all the seamen were given shore leave for the evening... with the exception of Adam."

Captain Oscarson picked up the story, "I knew your father did not want Adam to leave the ship. I called to him to get out of line of the men waiting to descend the rope ladder to the dinghy to take them ashore." With more assertion in his voice, he said, "Adam went berserk and fought like a tiger to go down the rope ladder. He pushed and shoved the men... well, there was quite a scuffle. I think all of the men wanted a piece of the action. After being cooped up on the ship for many days, my men were eager for a little excitement... and Adam was a worthy opponent. He fought with determination... I'll say that. He had to get off this ship."

"Yes, well, I know why he fought with such determination," General Von volunteered. "He knew I had figured out that he was the one in my office who had sold crucial information to Sun Lo regarding the logistics for the kidnapping. He's avoiding me for good reason."

"I can understand his reasoning." Captain Oscarson acknowledged and reported, "He is staying in his cabin because he is nursing many bruises and a couple of cracked ribs. In fact, the galley cook says he is in a lot of pain." The captain nonchalantly said, "I guess I didn't call off my men soon enough."

General Von assured the captain, "He deserved everything he got and much more. I'll be happy when I turn him over to the harbor police in Hong Kong."

"We're scheduled to pull into Victoria Harbor late this afternoon. You won't have to wait much longer." The captain responded.

*****

It was a beautiful sight to see the skyline of Hong Kong as the ship approached Victoria Harbor. Vessels of all descriptions were anchored and small sampans circled the water as the *Ladybug* negotiated a birth at the wharf near Kowlon.

Rachel and General Von stood on deck marveling at the welcoming sound of activity both in the harbor and on the dock. Even the pungent odor from the harbor was not repugnant to their nose. The two weary travelers were happy to be in China after a long, grueling experience.

"What a beautiful day," Rachel repeated to her father, and with a happy lilt in her voice, she tenderly held his arm and softly whispered, "Let's go home. I want to see all my little friends in the orphanage."

"Good idea!" General Von gave his daughter a big hug and turned to Captain Oscarson, "For the first time, I am speechless to think of the appropriate words to express my thanks for everything. I think the positive forces of feng shui were with us all the way from Canton to Yokohama and back to Hong Kong." He pondered their chances of ever meeting again and asked, "How can I repay you?"

"Well, ol' friend, that's easy," Captain Oscarson responded. "Next year when I come to Hong Kong, you can buy me a good, expensive dinner at the Peninsula Hotel in Kowlon. And, let's hope our meeting will be under happier circumstances."

"Done!" General Von happily agreed.

The two men shook hands and said their good-byes.

The gangplank was lowered quickly and Rachel and General Von were the first to disembark. They turned to wave to Captain Oscarson and noticed Adam... handcuffed and shackled, stumbling down the gangplank escorted by the harbor police.

CHAPTER FORTY-THREE

The irritating buzz from the alarm clock awoke Rachel from a deep sleep in her own bed. She lazily stretched her body under the covers with a feeling of security... happy to be home. Usually, the alarm bristled her temperament into a sensitive mood, as she hated the sound... thinking it was the worst sound she had ever heard. Now, she believes the worst sound is the frightening, deafening sound of a tsunami. She realizes there will be many things that she will look at differently as a result of her experiences over the past few weeks. She slowly looked around her bedroom fully appreciating her freedom of life.

Rachel anticipated a day filled with happiness as she planned to be with the little children in the orphanage. She quickly dressed in the typical Chinese garments, putting on loose-fitting black trousers with the customary apron hanging in front and back to the ankles and a long black jacket, which reached to her knees. She tied her long, blonde hair back with a ribbon and glanced into the dresser mirror. She was surprised to see she had lost a lot of weight, but her body was still curvaceous and she was pleased with the new, slimmer figure. She stood longer looking into the mirror and was saddened with the thought that she would never again wear this style clothing in her new life.

The general was already seated in the living room waiting for Rachel as the two were going to surprise the children at breakfast.

They crossed the open courtyard to the dining hall, opened the door and with a burst of yells from the little children, they were quickly surrounded. Some children had big grins on their face, while others cried with happiness. They hugged Rachel and followed her to the table as if she were the "Pied Piper of Hamelin".

After everyone had eaten a hearty breakfast, the children were eager to hear where Rachel had been and they wanted to hear her story. On occasion, General Von would tell them a fairy tale, but today, they wanted to hear what kept Rachel away from them for such a long time. Rachel moved her chair to the center of the dining hall and all the children sat on the floor in a circle around her. She felt as if she could cry looking at all the sweet expressions on their faces and decided to tell her story as a parable to "Sleeping Beauty". She definitely did not want the children to become frightened for her upon hearing the true facts of her kidnapping.

She began: "In the fairy tale 'Sleeping Beauty'… you all know the story very well… you remember the princess slept for a hundred years and was awakened by a kiss from her prince charming. Something similar happened to me. Although I was not asleep, I was kept against my will in a gloomy, old room until my 'prince' came from Korea to rescue me."

She elaborated upon the story to the delight of the children, weaving in certain elements, which made it sound like a tale of two lovers. As she developed the story, it became easier for her to tell the children that she was going to leave China and fly to the States where she would live happily ever after with her 'prince'. The dining hall became extremely quiet when she ended the beautiful, moving story. The children's emotions were mixed with happiness that she was going to marry her 'prince' and with sadness that she was going to leave the orphanage.

There was no school in celebration of Rachel's homecoming. Rachel spent the whole day with the children she had come to love as she knew this chapter in her life was coming to an end.

*****

Candle in the Window

General Von's life in the compound was now dedicated to his work in preparing the men for a huge drug bust in Hong Kong. His office had been alerted that another member of Yen Tso's Triad had taken over the operation and was working quickly to establish himself as the new leader. While his responsibilities demanded his time, pulling him away from further conversations with his daughter, Rachel was busy packing for her trip to the States. She was fortunate to have spent a few days alone with her father aboard ship making travel arrangements for her flight to Virginia. She will always treasure those few days they spent together.

It was decided that she should leave China quickly in order to prepare for her wedding on the plantation. The biggest thrill of the evening was her phone conversation with BillyJoe, her future father-in-law.

BillyJoe answered the phone: "Hello."

"Hello, BillyJoe, this is Rachel!"

"Rachel, honey!" He exploded. "Where are you? It's been a couple of months since I've received a letter from you or Seth. I've been worried sick. What's happened?"

Rachel could hear the worry in his high-pitched voice, "Don't worry about anything. We are both fine. Seth helped to rescue me from my abductors and we all survived the tsunami in Japan, and Seth has returned to Korea," she quickly reported.

"Hells bells, Rachel! Excuse my French, but please don't lay that on me without explaining it. What are you talking about? And you don't want me to worry?" BillyJoe scolded.

"It's a very long story and I want to tell you everything when I come to Virginia. The really good news is that Seth and I are going to be married on the plantation as soon as he is mustered out of the army, which we figure should be in six months," she happily responded. "And, I'm catching a plane tomorrow for Virginia and I'd appreciate it if you would meet me at the airport day after tomorrow."

"Of course," BillyJoe said. "You sure have given me a lot to think about... without telling me very much. I guess I can wait a couple of days to hear the whole story. I'm happy to hear you and Seth are safe and are getting married. I kind of figured you would get married some day and it's great the wedding will be here." The phone started to crackle as if the line were going to be disconnected and he quickly injected, "I'll see you at the airport."

As was an old habit, BillyJoe walked to the kitchen cabinet to get a bottle of bourbon. He really needed a drink after that very short, terrifying, enlightening conversation, which only added more concern for Seth. He turned at the cabinet and remembered he gave up drinking a couple of years ago. Old habits are hard to break and he was determined not to give into the temptation. He sat alone at the kitchen table with his head in his hands… worried about his son in Korea.

*****

The flight was long, which included stops in Hawaii and San Francisco before the plane touched down onto the tarmac in Virginia. All the passengers applauded the smooth landing. BillyJoe greeted Rachel with a big hug and led the way through the terminal to the baggage carousel.

"There it is!" Rachel called as she pointed a finger.

"What? You have only one piece of luggage?" BillyJoe asked surprised.

"That's right. I'm starting a new life in a new country and I want new clothes." She responded. "Is Hannah still working for us in the office? I plan to ask her to show me around the city… you know, the best shops, where I can get my hair cut and styled… and all those good 'girl' things."

"You can take the car, and I know she will be happy to go shopping with you. She got married a few months ago and she probably knows all the good shops."

"Oh, BillyJoe, I don't know how to drive."

"Well, we can sure fix that quick. I'll teach you right away and then you can buy your own new car."

Rachel settled back in the car seat while BillyJoe drove. Her new life was already feeling like a wonderful dream. She marveled at the scenery along the way to the plantation and thought, *spring is a glorious time of year in Virginia.* Trees were bursting with new green foliage and flowers dotted the landscape in carpets of yellow and purple. Rachel had forgotten how beautiful the stately mansion was as it commanded a majestic view from the hill overlooking the meadow and lake.

She and BillyJoe sat for hours in the swing on the veranda enjoying the afternoon together. Rachel shared her story while BillyJoe sat quietly the whole time… totally absorbed by the spellbinding adventure. His brow grew deeper in wrinkles as the story unfolded. In retrospect, he felt better that he did not know what was happening during the months when he did not hear from Rachel or Seth as he would have worried himself into a nervous breakdown.

The afternoon sun faded late into evening and BillyJoe suggested that he would report on the operation and finances of the business later when Rachel had a chance to rest from the trip.

After a goodnight's sleep, Rachel awoke with a peaceful expression on her face… amazed with the thought: *In a very short time I have slept in four different beds: a horrible, dirty cot in the cell; a rocking bed on the ship; my bed at home in China; and now I am in my new bed in a beautifully decorated bedroom. Life keeps getting better.*

CHAPTER FORTY-FOUR

... six months later

Jubilation. Many soldiers in camp were packing their duffel bag for the last time. They had enough points to fulfill the requirement to end their tour of duty. For them, the war was over. They were going HOME. For Seth, this was the most beautiful word in the English language. He believed it signified a rebirth of life, conjuring up every emotion in his body and mind making all his senses sharp. He was going home to be married.

Seth was packed in short time and headed for the command tent. Major Tamermia was working at his desk when Seth entered. He saluted the major and said, "Corporal Coleman reporting, sir."

The major looked up, "Yes. I want to wish you a safe trip back to the States and I want to be the first to congratulate you on your forthcoming marriage."

"Thank you, sir," Seth responded.

"I am very proud of the way you acquitted yourself in the field during the fire fights, and I appreciate your fine work as the court clerk. I believe this war has made a man of you, corporal. You remind me of my younger brother. I'll miss you."

"Sir, I am very proud to have served under your command."

They stood silently for a few minutes not knowing what to say; and realizing they may never see one another again, the major stepped forward extending his hand to Seth in a long, warm handshake. Seth stood proud and tall, showing great respect for the major, saluted, and left the tent.

"Man, where have you been?" Ian called. "You're going to miss the ride."

"I'd never miss this ride," Seth said with a big smile on his face. "We're going home!"

The roar of the engine of the old truck was a joyous sound as the raucous soldiers waved good-bye to their friends in camp. It was a bumpy, festive ride all the way to Inchon, Korea, where the soldiers boarded the *Marine Lynx,* which took them directly to Seattle, Washington. There was laughing, cheering, and a lot of hoopla during the sixteen-day voyage with no one giving any disparaging thought to the swinging hammocks stacked high for sleeping. The sound of the anchor hitting against the hull of the ship at the bow during rough water did not disturb the soldiers. They were herded like cattle… but no one really cared. They were going home.

The ship's arrival in Seattle was a sight that Seth would never forget. Fire boats sprayed water in the air from hoses; horns and whistles screeched; crowds of people at the dock pushed forward trying to touch the hand of a soldier. It appeared everyone in Seattle wanted to welcome them home.

From Seattle, the soldiers flew to Camp Carson, Colorado, where they were issued new clothes… and then Seth flew to Virginia.

*****

"Seth, Seth, over here!" Rachel joyously called.

Seth pushed his way through the passengers at the gate, scanning the crowd for Rachel. The terminal was quite crowded and Rachel had to call again before he saw her.

They embraced and kissed… happy to be together.

"I have a surprise for you," Rachel volunteered.

"What's that?" Seth responded.

"Do you see that new blue car parked close to the curb in the lot?"

"Yes."

"I just bought it. I know how to drive!" Rachel yelled with enthusiasm.

"Do I dare ride with you?" Seth teased.

"Of course! Let's go home."

*****

BillyJoe sat in the swing on the veranda waiting to welcome Seth home. It was difficult for him to contain his feelings; and when he embraced his son, his eyes filled with fatherly tears. Rachel decided to leave the two alone to visit while she finalized the wedding arrangements.

The wedding was scheduled for a time that would leave them five days for last-minute chores. Seth had to rent a tuxedo and buy some new clothes; out-of-town guests were expected to arrive in three days and... well, everything was left to the capable wedding planner.

*****

The day of the wedding was spectacular. Caterers hustled to set the tables, prepare the food and chill the champagne for the reception; florists arrived to decorate the atrium in beautiful fall colors with cascading flowers hanging from the circular staircase; chairs were placed in the atrium where the wedding nuptials took place, and the entire patio was covered with a large white canopy with hanging Japanese lanterns illuminating the dining tables and dance floor.

Rachel looked absolutely beautiful when she appeared on the balcony wearing a pure silk white wedding dress with a chapel-length train and a cathedral veil. The gown softly flowed as she gracefully descended the circular staircase to the atrium. The scene was picture perfect when General Von took his place at the foot of the staircase waiting to escort his daughter down the aisle.

Seth savored every moment of the ceremony. He thought, *if this is a dream, I never want to wake up.*

At the bride and groom's request, the musicians played the last song of the evening, while Rachel softly sang to Seth: "Because of you there's a song in my heart, because of you my romance had it's start. Because of you the sun will shine; the moon and stars will all be mine, forever and ever...."

It was the end to a long, grand, glorious day when the guests left the reception tired and happy. The two lovers slowly ascended the circular staircase to the bedroom where Seth picked up Rachel to carry her over the threshold. They were oblivious to anything and everything in the whole world. Their world was being alone... together.

"I don't think a lifetime is going to be long enough for loving you." Seth murmured.

Seth was the first to pull away from a passionate kiss. "Ya know what, Rachel?"

"Yes, I know. You love me." Rachel sweetly answered.

"No. I'm crazy about you."

Seth rolled over and turned out the lamp on the nightstand... leaving only a soft glow from the candle in the window.

ABOUT THE AUTHOR

Jeannine Dahlberg was educated at the University of Missouri at Columbia, and Washington University at St. Louis. She combines her experience as a writer and her knowledge of foreign travel to tell a story with passion. She is also the author of *Riding the Tail of the Dragon*. She lives in St. Louis, Missouri.